The Magic Cloak

The Talisman - Book I

The Magic Cloak

Michael Harling

Copyright 2021
by Michael Harling

ISBN: 979-8-9907389-1-1

Published in the US and UK in 2024
by Lindenwald Press

All rights reserved. No part of this publication
may be reproduced, stored in, or introduced into,
a retrieval system, or transmitted, in any form, or
by any means (electronic, mechanical, photocopying,
recording, or otherwise), without the prior written
permission of the publisher.

Lindenwald LP Press

*To Mitch and Charlie
Without whom there would be no story.*

Also by Michael Harling

Postcards From Across the Pond
More Postcards From Across the Pond
Postcards From Ireland
Finding Rachel Davenport

Chapter 1
June 2013

This wasn't when the story began, but it's how it started for me.

Whizzzzzz, thunk.

"Strike one," Mr. Jennings said. "Keep your eye on the ball, son. And don't flinch."

I wiped a sheen of sweat from my forehead and adjusted the over-sized batting helmet. "It was going to hit me."

"Pussy," Pete, the kid behind the catcher's mask, said.

He threw the ball back to Bobby and went into his crouch, holding his mitt up to catch the next ball. I glance behind him, at Mr. Jennings, who folded his beefy arms and rested them on his stomach. "Just swing at the damn thing, okay?" Further beyond, sitting on a weathered bench, the rest of the boys snickered. Charlie was with them, but he wasn't snickering. He just rolled his eyes and looked up at the cloudless sky.

I settled the bat on my shoulder and turned to face Bobby, who made a show of eyeing me up.

Pete chuckled. "Just toss it underhand, Bobby," he said. "This guy can't hit."

Bobby threw the ball. I jumped aside.

Whizzzzzz, thunk.

This time, I swear I felt a breeze as the ball zipped by my elbow.

"What is your problem," Mr. Jennings said.

"Strike two," Pete said. "That's his problem."

"It was going to hit me."

"If I wanted you to eat the ball," Bobby shouted from the pitcher's mound, "it would already be halfway down your throat."

I glared at Bobby. He was a big kid with a buzz-cut, pink face and a dirty tee shirt that strained over his stomach.

"You'd probably eat it first," I muttered.

Bobby's face went a darker shade of pink. "What was that?"

Pete laughed and threw the ball to him. "He said you were fat."

"I did not!"

The snickering notched up and the kid on second base laughed. Bobby turned and looked at him and the laughing stopped.

"You calling me a liar?" Pete asked.

I couldn't read his expression through the mask, but I didn't think he was smiling. "Well, you lied, so, yeah, I guess."

"You don't need to worry about Bobby making you eat that ball—"

"Enough," Mr. Jennings said. He pulled a handkerchief from his pocket and mopped his face with it. "Just swing at the ball, son. Is that too much to ask?"

"It was going to hit me!"

He sighed and put the handkerchief away. "Just swing. That's all you gotta do."

"But—"

"You wanna come out here and say that to me?" Bobby shouted.

The snickering grew louder. Mr. Jennings' face grew red.

"Stop it. Now," he shouted. Silence returned to the ballpark, leaving only the sound of distant traffic and the smell of sun-baked dirt. Mr. Jennings pointed toward the pitcher's mound. "Bobby, pitch to this kid, and if you hit him, you're off the team."

Bobby's mouth dropped open, but before he got a chance to say anything, Mr. Jennings pointed at me. "And you, son, you swing at that pitch. And if you flinch again, I'll hit you with the ball. Got that?"

I felt my face go red. Bobby wound up. The park remained silent. All eyes were on me. Just what I wanted, everyone's undivided attention.

Whizzzzzz, thunk.

I swung as hard as I could, even though I knew I had already missed the ball. The momentum carried me, spinning me in an awkward circle until I tripped over my own feet and sprawled in the dirt. My helmet clattered away as my face hit the ground. I don't know where the bat ended up. The park erupted in laughter.

"Maybe baseball isn't your game," Mr. Jennings said.

I stood up, dusting off my shorts. "That's what I tried to tell my dad."

"But your twin brother, Charlie, is it? Is he going to try out?"

"He's not my twin."

Mr. Jennings scowled. "But you're …"

"Yes, we're both twelve, but we're not twins."

I hated this conversation. It was an easy assumption to make because we both had blue eyes and red hair—

though mine leaned more toward "carrot" while Charlie's was closer to chestnut. The fact that the similarity ended there didn't stop people asking, though, so this conversation happened a lot. But that wasn't why I hated it. I hated it because of what I knew Mr. Jennings was going to say next.

"Well, your older brother, then—"

"He's the younger one."

The laughter died down as the kids on the bench began fidgeting and the outfielders started pacing. Mr. Jennings looked around.

"Listen up, everyone," he shouted, clapping his hands for attention. "We'll break for lunch. Come back at two. We'll finish the batting and work on fielding."

Kids started picking up bats and gloves and helmets and the outfielders began walking in. Bobby strolled straight toward me."

"Ask him, will you?" Mr. Jennings said, already preoccupied. "I think he'd be an asset to the team."

I nodded but he had already turned away. Bobby was close now. Leaving seemed like it would be a good idea but as I stepped back, I bumped into someone. "A liar, am I?"

Pete spun me around and gripped my arm. Then another kid, Jason, the first baseman, grabbed my other arm.

"Hey!"

I struggled to pull away, but it was useless. They were older boys, already on the team, and stood a head taller than me, with more muscle. Then a sweaty hand thumped down on my shoulder.

"Wanna call me fat to my face?"

The three of them stood around me, crowding me, hemming me in.

"I didn't," I said, my voice sounding strained and whiny even to myself.

Pete punched my arm. "So, you're callin' me a liar!"

"C'mon, Mitch, let's go home."

They all looked toward Charlie, who came and stood about three feet away.

"Beat it, Wyman," Bobby said. "This doesn't concern you."

"What doesn't concern me?"

"Your little brother called me fat," Bobby said.

Pete punched my arm again. "And he called me a liar."

One side of Charlie's mouth curved into a smile. He shook his head. "Jesus, Mitch, you've been busy." Then he looked at Jason. "What did he do to you?"

Jason scowled. "Nothing."

"So, this doesn't concern you, either."

"They're my friends, so it concerns me."

"And Mitch is my brother, so it concerns me too."

The three of them stared at him. The lines were drawn, and it didn't look good. The two of us were no match for the three of them. In fact, the two of us were no match for any one of them. But Charlie just stood there with a half-smile on his face. Then he reached between Pete and Jason and pulled me by the arm.

"C'mon. It's time to go home."

Bobby grabbed me by the back of the neck, but then his hand fell away. When I looked back, Mr. Jennings was there, his hand on Bobby's shoulder.

"Thanks for your help this morning, guys," he said. "See you back here at two o'clock, right?"

They all murmured in agreement.

"And Charlie, are you coming back? You didn't get a chance to bat."

"I'm thinking about it," Charlie said, as we continued to distance ourselves from Bobby and his gang.

We kept walking. I strained to keep myself from looking back. Mr. Jennings wasn't going to stay with them forever. When we got to the road, I felt a wave of relief. Then Bobby shouted after us.

"Watch your back, Wyman. I know where you live."

Chapter 2

Wynantskill, New York is a small town, and the park—where the ballfield is—sits just about in the middle of it. Our house hugged the edge, on a quiet road with only a few other houses. Chain-link fences ran between the houses and the woods behind them, and, unlike the houses in town, our backyard was really big. Dad complained about having to mow it, but I could tell he liked the space. And so did I. It was a great place to play, and the woods were an exciting mystery to explore and pretend we were on expeditions, or warriors tracking an enemy.

But that was when we were younger, before I found I liked reading better than pretending, and before Dad started worrying that I was reading too much. Which was why—on the first day of what should have been a long and relaxing summer—I'd found myself trying out for the baseball team, and why I knew he was going to be very disappointed.

We found Dad, and Mom, on the back porch; Mom on a chaise longue with a book and Dad sitting in the big wicker chair with a bottle of Budweiser, making sweat-rings on the glass-top table. He looked our way and smiled as we thumped up the steps.

"How did it go?"

"I didn't get to bat yet," Charlie said, flopping onto the other chaise.

I sat on the porch railing. Dad looked at me.

"I didn't make the team."

He frowned. "Why not?"

I felt my stomach clench. "I can't throw, I can't catch, and I can't hit."

That was when I saw it, the disappointment, as his face lost all animation.

"C'mon, Mitch. You must be good at something."

"Trust him, Dad," Charlie said. "I'm a witness."

Dad took a sip of beer and set the bottle down, making another sweat ring. "Can't you go back, try again? Maybe I can talk to Jennings, see if he can—"

"No," I said, a little too forcefully.

Dad's brow furrowed. "Now look, Mitch, I'm not going to have you sitting around—"

"Leave it, Tom," Mom said. She had put her book down, closed, on her lap. There was no bookmark in it. "You can't force him to be good at baseball."

Dad's jaw tightened, but he took a deep breath and a swig of beer, and when he looked at me again, he seemed only half as disappointed.

"Tell you what," he said. "I heard there's going to be a super full moon tonight. Why don't we get your old telescope out and have a good look at it?"

I knew he wanted to look at the moon about as much as I wanted to play baseball, but he was making an effort, so I mumbled, "Sure, that'd be great."

He took another sip of beer to fill the awkward silence that followed. Then he smiled. "I was going to save this for later," he said, "but maybe now is the right time."

"Tom," Mom said, "we agreed."

"What's the harm," Dad said. "Wait here, I'll be back in a sec with a nice surprise."

He went into the house. The screen door banged behind him. Mom shook her head. "Your grandfather sent you something."

"What for?" Charlie asked. "And why now?"

"Who knows," Mom said.

"He couldn't be bothered to send us Christmas presents."

"He sent gift cards," I reminded him.

The screen door banged open. Dad came out carrying a cardboard box with a Hewlett-Packard logo on it. I expected it was a re-used box. I couldn't imagine Granddad sending an ink-jet printer all the way from England. He set it down between me and Charlie. Our address was scrawled on it in black marker. There was no return address.

"This better not be Mitch's birthday present," Charlie said. "All I got was a lousy card."

"It's too early," I said, "and besides, it's addressed to both of us."

"Why would he do that?" Charlie asked.

Dad seemed more excited than either of us. "Open it and find out."

"All this time," Mom said, "and suddenly he dumps this on us. What's he up to."

Dad shook his head and sat back down at the table. "He's not up to anything. He's simply staying in touch," he said, taking another sip of beer.

Mom put her book on the floor and stood up. "By not telling us where he lives? By not giving us an email address or a phone number?"

"He's only been over there a little while, maybe he's still settling in."

Mom put her hands on her hips. "It's been months," she said, her voice rising. "It's like he's hiding

9

from us."

Dad sighed. "He's not hiding. He's—"

"What, finding himself?"

"So what if he is? It's no business of ours."

"He's my children's grandfather and he's disappeared from their lives."

Dad stood up. His chair banged against the side of the house. "And he's my father, and in case you've forgotten, he's the reason we're in this house, and the reason we can sit on this porch, so if he wants to go off on a spiritual discovery, I think we can all cut him some slack."

"What the hell?"

We all looked at Charlie as he began pulling dark blue material out of the box like a magician doing the handkerchief trick. Mom and Dad were so stunned they didn't even tell him to watch his language.

"What is this, a bedspread?" Charlie asked, pulling more material out. "How are we supposed to share a bedspread?"

I grabbed a handful and helped him. It was thick and heavy; but soft, like velvet. We dumped the material on the porch floor, then looked in the box in case that was the packing, and the real gift was still inside.

"Nope, no Xbox," Charlie said.

There was only a piece of paper. I picked it up.

"It's from Granddad," I said.

Dad came over and poked at the mound of material. Then he lifted it by an edge. It was as long as he was tall.

"Read it," Dad said. "Maybe he'll tell us."

I unfolded the letter, skimming over the hellos and how are yous. "Um, he's settling in … he's living in some place called Horsham … the weather's fine … ah, here it is. He says, 'I found this in a quirky charity shop a short walk from where I live. The shop is run by an old man who never seems to sell anything, but he has an eclectic collection of curious objects, so I like to poke my nose in there on occasion. It was he who pointed this out to me'."

I looked up. Dad was still examining the material. It was oddly shaped and didn't look like a blanket. "Doesn't he say what 'this' is?"

"Hang on," I said, "there's more. 'He told me it appeared in his shop a long time ago; one day it wasn't there, and the next it was, along with an ancient parchment containing mysterious verses. The old man couldn't tell me anything more about it other than the obvious: it's magic. And what better gift to send to two imaginative young boys than a Magic Cloak?'"

I looked up from the letter. "A cloak?"

Charlie shook his head. "Magic? He must be loopy. We're not six anymore."

Then I looked at Mom. She was staring, open-mouthed, her face white as the paper I was holding. She put a hand against the wall to steady herself. "You will not have that."

"What?" Charlie said.

Dad dropped the cloak and went to her. "Donna, are you all right?"

She pushed past him, pointing at the cloak. "You give that to me."

Charlie stepped in front of it. "Granddad gave it to us."

Dad tried to hold Mom back. "What is wrong with you?"

"It's not a toy. It's not for them."

"Uh, yeah, it is," Charlie said.

Mom glared at him. "Don't you—"

"No," Dad said, so sharply we all went silent. "Don't you. My father sent his grandsons a gift. Yeah, it's strange. Yeah, he's gone a little off the rails. But that doesn't give you the right—"

Mom shook her head, her hands squeezing her temples. "You don't understand."

"There's nothing to understand. It's theirs."

Mom's face became more pink than white as she took a few deep breaths. "You do not leave this property," she said, pointing at me and Charlie. "And you do nothing with that ... that cloak."

She yanked the door open and stalked into the house, slamming the door behind her. Dad sighed, shook his head, and followed.

Then the shouting started.

Chapter 3

"You're such a doormat," Charlie said.

We'd left the porch to sit at the end of the back yard, far enough from the house that we couldn't hear what was going on inside. Charlie had brought the cloak, dragging it along behind him, to keep it out of Mom's reach. It now laid in a heap in front of where we sat, cross-legged, in the shade of the trees.

The buzzing in my stomach had started to subside, but I was a long way from feeling calm.

"How can I not be a doormat?" I asked. "Bobby's three times my size. He's going to walk all over me no matter what I do."

Charlie shook his head. "I meant with Mom."

"Mom's not gonna beat me up."

"Neither is Blobby Bobby. Just stay out of his way. By tomorrow he'll have found someone else to torment."

I picked up a twig and snapped it in half, and then into quarters. He was probably right. There was nothing personal between Bobby and me, no history, no bad blood. I was just a smaller kid, and he was a bigger kid, and that gave him the right to pound on me until he found someone else to pound on. I would have felt better if he at least knew my name; I wasn't a person, I was just a target. It wasn't fair, and there was nothing I could do about it.

I tossed the bits of twig aside and picked up a bigger one. Charlie plucked a stone off the ground and threw it over the fence into the woods. I snapped the twig and wondered what was happening inside the house.

"Why is Mom so upset about Granddad?" I asked. "All he did was move away. Sure, it's strange he's gone off-grid, but it's not like he's her dad."

Charlie shrugged. "She's a control freak. Granddad's done something. She doesn't like it. Someone has to pay. But it's not going to be me."

"I didn't know you wanted a cloak so badly."

Charlie laughed. "It's the worst gift anyone has ever given me. But I wasn't going to let her take it."

I stood and picked the cloak up. It was too big for me to see the whole thing, even when I held one end up as far as I could, so I laid it out on the ground. It was sort of fan-shaped, with a collar and an ornate, silver clasp. Sticking out of a seam in the collar was a piece of paper. I fished it out, taking care not to damage it.

"Look," I said, holding up a small scroll. It was yellowed with age and crackled as I unrolled it.

Charlie peered over my shoulder. "What is it?"

"Dunno." I squinted at the spindly, florid writing. "It's a poem, I think. It says, 'This transmigrating robe will send, its wearer there and back again …' It must be the mysterious verse the old man found when the cloak appeared in his shop."

Charlie laughed. "Granddad got this at a garage sale, and he made up that stupid poem. Mom's right, he is off his rocker."

I put the scroll in my pocket. "At least he's making an effort."

I pulled the cloak around my shoulders and fastened

the clasp. The bottom swirled around my feet like a velvet pool.

"Playing dress up, are we?"

My stomach turned to ice. It was Bobby.

Charlie and I spun around. Pete and Jason were there too, flanking Bobby. They were twenty feet away, approaching at a fast walk.

I unclasped the cloak, dropped it to the ground and stepped in front of it. Charlie stood next to me.

"What do we do?" I asked.

Before we could think of anything, they fanned out and raced toward us. Charlie ran to the side, but Jason cut him off and grabbed him in a headlock.

"Let me go, asshole."

Jason gripped him tighter. "This doesn't concern you or me, so let's just sit this one out."

He spun Charlie around, so he was facing my way. I stayed where I was. It was no use running. Pete grabbed me in a head lock. Bobby came close, leering down at me. I glanced at the house hoping Mom might come out to call us for lunch. Bobby followed my gaze.

"Gonna call for mommy and daddy? That's what cry-babies do." He grabbed my face and squeezed, forcing my mouth into fish-lips. "Are you gonna cry, Wyman, or should I say, Whine-man? That's a good name for you. I think I'll have everyone call you Whine-man from now on because you're such a baby."

My cheeks burned at the thought. And when school started, it might even spill over onto Charlie, and it would be my fault. Bobby would do it too. It was personal now. I liked it better when I was an anonymous target.

"Two of you against a kid half your size," Charlie shouted. "Who's the baby?"

Jason shook him. Charlie struggled. Bobby ignored them. Then he looked at the cloak.

"What's this?" He said, picking it up.

"Leave that alone," I said.

"Hmm, valuable, is it? Something you wouldn't want to lose?"

My mouth went dry. I'd figured he was going to slap me around a bit, maybe make me eat some dirt. But if we lost the cloak, Mom would kill us.

"I think this will be a lot more fun than dealing with these assholes." He said, walking toward the fence.

"Bring that back."

I heard him grunt as he climbed over the fence. Footsteps rustled in the leaves as he walked further into the woods. "C'mon, you two," he called.

Pete pushed me to the ground. I tried to get up to go after Bobby, but Pete landed on my back, his knees on my shoulder blades. My breath whooshed out and left me paralyzed. Pete jumped up and ran. I struggled to breathe, but all I could do was make a sound like, "Huh, huh, huh."

"Mitch," Charlie called. "Are you all right?"

I lifted my head. "Huh, huh."

"Let go of me, you bastard."

I heard a thud as Charlie's body hit the ground. Then Jason jumped the fence and ran into the woods after Pete and Bobby.

"Mitch, are you okay?"

Charlie was at my side. I shook my head. "Huh, wind … knocked … out …"

I took a shuddering breath. Charlie helped me sit up. I breathed deeper.

"I'm … okay … now," I said.

My ribs ached, but they didn't seem broken. If they

had been, I was sure they would have hurt more.

"Then, come on."

"What?"

"We're going after that cloak."

"But—"

It was too late. Charlie was already gone. I climbed to my feet in time to see him disappear into the trees. I sighed and followed.

Chapter 4

By the time I caught up with Charlie, we were well out of sight of the house. The woods weren't really a forest, they were just a few acres of trees, but they were thick and the ground, in places, was covered in undergrowth. I wasn't worried about getting lost, though. We had spent years exploring and knew our way around, so that wasn't the problem. The problem was, we needed to find Bobby, and even if we knew the woods better than he did, there were too many places to hide.

We raced blindly through the trees, further and further from the house, chasing sounds we hoped might be Bobby, Pete, or Jason, but it was useless. After a while I stopped. Silence.

"Smart move," I said, leaning against a tree, panting. "Now we've lost the cloak and we've left the yard. If Mom looks out the window, we're toast."

A kaleidoscope of shade, sunshine, leaves, trees, and bushes surrounded us, but there was no sign of Bobby, or the cloak.

Charlie shook his head in disgust. "You're right. We should go back. Mom can't be mad if we tell her the truth. And I don't care about telling on Bobby. Being a bully is one thing, but stealing is another. We should be able to get the cloak back, even if it means calling the police."

"But by then, who knows what he'll have done to it."

Charlie shrugged. "It's Mom who'll go after him to get the cloak back. He's welcome to it as far as I'm concerned."

We took a step in the direction of the house, then heard rustling in the bushes ahead of us.

We froze.

"Shit," Charlie said.

"What?"

"Bobby's not stealing the cloak, he's using it as bait."

Pete and Jason broke cover, charging our way. We turned and ran.

They were well behind us, and our knowledge of the woods gave us an advantage, but we still couldn't lose them. We dodged around bushes and jumped over fallen logs while they shouted and blundered through the forest, not making any attempt to conceal themselves. When we ran to the right, we heard one of them coming at us from that direction, so we ran left, and then the other would come at us. We ran a zig-zag pattern, always moving deeper into the woods, which was the opposite direction we wanted to go in.

"They're herding us," Charlie said, "pushing us into a trap."

"What can we do?"

We zigged, then zagged, moving closer to wherever it was they wanted us to go.

"There's a ravine ahead," Charlie said. "If we can get to that, we can use it as cover to work our way around and come up behind them."

I knew the place he meant. We ran toward it, cresting a small rise and then descending into a shallow valley. "This way," Charlie said.

We ran as quietly as we could, keeping low, hoping to pass by whoever it was chasing us. Behind us came a thud and a rustle of branches as someone else jumped into the ravine. We turned to look, but they were too far away for us to see. They had simply wanted us to know they were there.

"Quick, back up the slope," Charlie said.

"What?"

"They want us to run this way," he said, turning around. "This is where the trap is."

I scanned the bushes and trees and rocks. So many places to hide. "We have to get out of here."

We scrambled for the side. I heard footsteps pounding the ground behind us, then everything went dark, and something pulled against my chest, dragging me back. One of my arms was pinned to my side, the other against Charlie. I kicked and squirmed, but it was no use.

"Let go, you asshole," Charlie shouted.

"I've got them. I've got them," Bobby shouted, squeezing us together so tight I struggled to breathe.

I tried to see what was happening, but everything was dark. We were wrapped in the cloak, with Bobby giving us a bear-hug.

"Let go!"

"Nu-uh," Bobby said. "We've got plans for you."

I struggled harder. We needed to escape before Pete and Jason arrived or we were going to be in for it.

For a second, I thought we were getting free. Bobby's grip slackened, then dropped altogether. I was so surprised it took me a second to move, and by then it was too late. Bobby's hand smacked me on the side of the face. Charlie's head jerked toward mine. A hollow thud reverberated through my skull and a bolt of light flashed in the darkness.

Then I tumbled to the ground, and everything went black.

Chapter 5
August 517 AD

My head throbbed. I opened my eyes. The cloak was still over us. I tensed, waiting for a kick or punch, but none came.

Cautiously, I pulled the cloak off, sat up and blinked. We were still in the woods, but not in the place where Bobby had ambushed us. We were no longer in the ravine, there were bushes all around us and a thick canopy of trees overhead.

Charlie sat up and moaned. "Where's Bobby?"

"I don't know."

"And how did we get here?"

"I don't know that either."

Charlie rubbed the side of his head. "Well, at least we're not getting beat up."

I stood up and waited for my head to stop spinning. "Maybe he was satisfied with knocking our heads together."

"Bobby? I doubt it. He and his buddies are probably hiding, waiting for us."

I picked up the cloak and rolled it into an awkward bundle. "If they are, there's not much we can do about it. We need to get home."

Charlie stood. "Then let's get out of here and see if anything looks familiar." He tried to make an opening by pushing the branches aside. "Ow! Those leaves are sharp."

I took a closer look. "These are holly bushes."

"As in 'Deck the Halls with Boughs of' bushes?"

I felt one of the leaves. It was dark green, leathery, and edged with spikes. "Yeah, but holly doesn't grow around here."

"It must," Charlie said, "because we're here, and this is holly."

"So, the question is, 'Where's here?'"

Charlie shook his head. "No, the question is, how do we get out of here?"

I looked around. We were in a solid circle of six-foot tall holly bushes. "There's no way out. Or in."

"We must have been knocked out cold for them to carry us to … wherever we are."

I dropped the cloak and sat on it. "No, none of this makes sense. Look at the sky."

We both craned our necks, looking up through the trees, which were thicker and older than the ones behind our house. The bits of sky showing between the leaves weren't blue, they were grey. "The sun was shining a minute ago. And it's cooler now."

"So? We must have been knocked out long enough for them to carry us here. And while we were out, it got cloudy."

"That's the thing," I said. "If we were knocked out for that long, we wouldn't be waking up here, we'd be waking up in intensive care."

Charlie rubbed his chin. "Well, we won't find any answers in here."

In the end, we had to wriggle under the lowest branches, which wasn't easy or pain-free. The spikes scratched our arms and legs and pulled at our tee shirts. I crawled after Charlie, pulling the cloak behind. When we were finally free, we stood up, brushed ourselves off and looked around at an unfamiliar setting.

"Where on earth are we?" Charlie asked.

As far as we could see, which wasn't all that far, there were broad oak trees, elms, a scattering of wild apple trees and a carpet of low shrubs covering the forest floor.

"There is nothing like this anywhere near where we live," I said. "And listen."

We stood still, holding our breath.

"What do you hear?"

Charlie shrugged. "Nothing."

"Exactly. No traffic, no airplanes. It's totally silent. We are nowhere near home."

Charlie looked to his left, then to his right. "I don't suppose you have your phone on you?"

Mom and Dad had presented me with a cell phone on my 12th birthday. They did the same for Charlie, but he'd already had his confiscated for joining a WhatsApp group with some other boys in his class, for the purpose of exchanging nudie pictures. I was pretty sure I had left mine on the dresser in my bedroom because I hadn't wanted to risk losing it at the baseball try-outs. Still, I patted my pockets, just in case.

"Hey, my wallet's gone."

"Mine too," Charlie said, slapping his backside. "Those bastards stole my wallet. I had twelve dollars in there."

I felt my other pockets. The scroll was still there, but nothing else.

"We've got to find a way out of here," Charlie said, an edge of panic in his voice.

I fought down my own fear and tried to think.

"The forest looks like it thins out in that direction,"

I said, pointing. "Let's try there."

Charlie said nothing. There was no other option. I struggled through the undergrowth, clutching the cloak to my chest, with Charlie following. After a few minutes, we could see larger patches of sky, but there was still no sign of a road, and no sound of traffic. Then we heard a faint hammering sound.

"Listen," I said, stopping so suddenly that Charlie ran into me. "It sounds like someone pounding in fence-posts or chopping wood."

Charlie pointed. "It's in that direction. Come on."

We stumbled through the bushes until, at last, the forest and undergrowth began to thin out, which made the going easier. Then, through the trees, we spotted a clearing, a rough circle of spiky grass and low stumps. On the far side was a stand of young trees, planted close together in neat rows. They were straight as signposts, and all the same height, with willowy branches reaching out to one another, making an unbroken haze of green. Next to a small pile of felled trees, was a boy chopping at them with an axe.

"Finally," Charlie said, rushing ahead. "Come on."

I struggled to keep up with him. When we got to the edge of the clearing, I grabbed his arm to stop him.

"What are you doing? Let go."

I squatted and tried to pull him down with me. "No. Look."

"Why? We've finally found—"

"Look!"

He stopped, then squatted next to me. The boy was dressed in something that looked like a smock with a length of rope for a belt. His axe was nothing but a sharp rock tied to a stick with leather strips. Hanging from his belt was a knife, but it wasn't made of metal.

It looked more like bone or hard wood.

"What do you make of that?"

Charlie shrugged. "A re-enactment?"

"Of what? This kid looks like someone out of the stone-age. And where are the other re-enactors? And have you heard of any re-enactments anywhere near us?"

"Well, all we can do is ask him."

I nodded. "I guess. But I still don't like this. There's something strange going on."

We stood and stepped into the clearing. The chopping noise had stopped. The boy was gone.

"Hey, where did he go?"

A strong arm gripped me around the neck. I barely had time to yelp before something sharp pressed against my throat.

"Stand where you are," a voice hissed in my ear. "State your business."

Chapter 6

I was too shocked to react. I dropped the cloak. My arms fell limp to my sides. Charlie's face went white. He raised his hands in front of him, palms out.

"Whoa," he said. "There's no need for that."

The arm tightened around my neck and the sharp edge pressed painfully against my windpipe. "Be still," the voice said, calmer this time. "Tell me who you are."

Charlie took a deep breath. "I'm Charlie," he said, his voice quivering, "and you're holding my brother, Mitch. Please let him go."

"Why are you spying? Did you come to rob me?"

"We're not thieves," I said, struggling to keep from choking, and from wetting myself. "We're lost. We just want to know the way home."

The pressure on my neck eased. "Thieves and scoundrels lurk in these woods," the voice said. Then a hand patted my sides. "You are not armed?"

"Of course not. Just let us go and point the way home," Charlie said, "and you'll never see us again."

The arm released me. I sank to the ground and skittered over to Charlie. Only then did I dare look back at the guy who attacked me. It was the boy, holding a wooden knife.

I gaped at him. He was no older than I was, but he had the strength of a full-grown man. Red hair—recently trimmed with garden shears, it seemed—fell to his shoulders and his strange shirt hung loosely around his lanky frame. He looked comical, but I was not tempted to laugh—he still had the knife and, although it was crude and made from some sort of hard wood, it seemed lethal enough.

The boy glared at us, eyeing our sneakers, our clothes, and our hair with what looked to me like suspicion mingled with confusion. Then his expression softened. "You do not look like thieves, but you dress strangely." He bent down and reached for the cloak. "And what is this?"

I grabbed it and pulled it away. "A blanket," I said. "It's ours."

"It looks a fine blanket." The suspicious expression returned. "How did you come by it?"

"Our grandfather gave it to us," I said.

The boy smirked. "Then your grandfather must be a wealthy man indeed to give such things away."

I stood next to Charlie; the cloak bundled against my chest. We both backed away. "Will you stop talking like that?"

"Like what?"

I sighed. "Like you're a peasant from the Middle Ages. I realize you want to stay in character, but we're really lost, and we need to get home."

"Where is your home?"

"Wynantskill," Charlie said.

The boy looked puzzled. "I know of no kingdom called Wynantskill. Is it far?"

"It's not a …" Charlie said, then he shook his head and crossed his arms. "Just tell us how to get to the nearest town, okay?"

The boy pointed in the direction we had been heading. "The town is that way, but you would be better going back to the road."

His words gave me a jolt of hope. "What road?"

"The road you were on," the boy said, his brow furrowing as he narrowed his eyes. "You must have come from that direction, there is no other way to get here."

"How do we get to the road," Charlie asked.

The boy shook his head. "The way you came."

"But we didn't come from the road," I said.

"You came from somewhere," the boy said. "You didn't just appear in the forest."

Charlie shrugged. "Well, actually, we kinda did."

The boy stepped back a few paces, holding the knife in front of him again. "You are playing me as a fool. Is this your game? To confound and rob me?"

"This is getting ridiculous," I said to Charlie. "He seems determined to remain in character."

Charlie rolled his eyes, then looked at the boy. "Are there any kids around here we can talk to?"

The boy's eyes widened. He held the knife out at arm's length. "Now you want to talk to goats? Are you demons?"

Charlie looked at me, raising his eyebrows. "Goats? Demons?"

"Calm down," I said. "We're just …" I was about to say, "kids," but I realized he must be pretending the word "kid" meant a young goat. "… boys, like you. And we're trying to get home. Can you help us? We mean you no harm."

I leaned toward Charlie. "If we play along," I whispered, "maybe he'll be more cooperative."

Charlie took a step toward the boy. "Look, we're friends, okay? We, um, come in peace. Just show us to the road and we'll be on our way."

The boy lowered the knife but kept his eyes on us. "I am working. I have no time to guide you."

Charlie looked at the sky, shaking his head. Then he looked at the boy. "Seriously," he said, his voice rising, "we're lost, we don't know where we are, we don't know where the road is, and we don't know how to get to town. Can't you cut us a break?"

The boy circled around us, keeping his eyes, and the knife, pointing our way. "I'm sorry. I need to finish here. When I do, you may follow me. But keep your distance."

"I know this isn't part of your script," I said, "but we're in a hurry."

The boy edged away, stepping slowly backward toward where we had first seen him working. "I can't return home until my work is done," he said. "Allow me to finish. The less you talk, the faster I can work."

Charlie looked at me. "What now?"

I watched the boy, who was no longer threatening us with his knife and was, instead, stripping branches from a sapling and glancing our way every few seconds. "I don't know. This kid is unstable. The stunt he pulled with the knife was well out of line. We ought to report him once we get out of here, but right now we need to keep him docile until we can find a responsible adult."

"Well, we better find one soon. Mom's gonna have a fit. She's probably called us for lunch already. She'll skin us when we get home."

"Maybe we can help him," I said. "If we join in his game, he might be more willing to cooperate."

We started moving slowly across the clearing, but not directly toward the boy.

"Make sure you keep some distance between us," I said, "and keep an eye on that knife."

"What are you doing?" the boy asked, as soon as we started moving.

We took another step forward. The boy dropped the sapling and backed away.

Charlie sighed and shook his head. "Will you get a grip? We're not going to hurt you. Just let us help you. If we help, you'll be done sooner."

The boy watched us as we continued to approach but didn't back away. He seemed to be deciding if he could trust us. Then he tucked the knife into his rope belt and picked up the axe. "As you wish," he said, resting the axe over his shoulder. He pointed to the saplings he had been stripping, and then to a pile of rods and a jumble of woven branches. "You can separate the withies from the staves. I will cut more trees."

As we approached, he backed away, into the rows of saplings, until he was nearly out of sight.

"Hey!" Charlie called after him. "What is your name?"

"Pendragon," the boy said.

Charlie smirked. "Of course it is."

Chapter 7

I put the cloak down and we looked at the piles of what the kid who called himself Pendragon had told us were staves and withies.

"What are we supposed to do?" Charlie asked.

"Do you mean, what are we supposed to do with these things, or how are we going to get out of here? In either case, I don't know." I shook my head trying to clear the confusion. None of what was happening made sense, and I couldn't force it to make sense. "All we can do is keep moving and hope we get somewhere."

"And how are we supposed to do that?"

I shrugged. "For a start, I guess we make staves and withies."

Charlie examined a sapling. "That's nuts. Mom is … somewhere, screaming for our hides while we're wasting time playing cave man with a lunatic."

"We need to forget about Mom for a while," I said. "We've been here, what, half an hour or more? And if this really is some elaborate joke, it took a long time to set up. Face it, Mom already knows we're gone. We've probably been gone for so long she's called the cops."

"I hope so," Charlie said. "This is getting ridiculous. And that kid isn't bothered at all about helping us."

"I think we should just play along for now. At some point, we'll find something familiar or someone to help us."

Charlie sighed. "Okay, but what's a stave and how do I make one?"

I looked at the saplings, and the items that Pendragon said he was making. "It looks like you strip the branches off the trees," I said, "and I strip the leaves off the branches."

"What for?"

"So we can feel like we're in the Middle Ages."

Charlie picked up one of the saplings. "This is stupid," he said, yanking at the branches, "I can't believe people do this for fun."

It was hard work without any tools and my hands were soon raw from pulling leaves and bending branches. Then, Pendragon returned, dragging another sapling with him. He threw it on top of the others and stood, watching us work, one hand on his hip and the other holding the axe. I got the feeling he was disappointed.

"Sorry we haven't done more," I said, stripping another branch, "but we're not as into this as you are."

"You've had your fun," Charlie said, twisting a branch, trying to break it off. "Can you show us the way home now?"

Pendragon looked at Charlie. "Friend," he said, sounding slightly alarmed, "this is not good for the stave." He put his hand over Charlie's to make him stop. "Are you so unskilled at—"

His eyes grew wide, and his jaw dropped.

"What?" Charlie asked.

"Your hands," he said.

I put the branch I was working on down and looked at mine. They were red and sore but otherwise unremarkable. "Yeah, and?"

Pendragon came to me and ran a calloused finger across my palm. "They are soft as a baby's." He stepped back, bowed, then knelt. "Forgive me, but you led me to believe … I did not know."

"Know what?" Charlie asked.

"You are high born. Please, I acted from ignorance. I meant no harm."

"Just stop it, will you," Charlie said, "and show us how to get out of here."

Pendragon stood, turned to Charlie and bowed again. "Yes, sires," he said. "At once."

He scuttled around, gathered the finished staves into a bundle, then tried binding them with twine, but his hands shook so much the knot slipped, spilling the bundle.

I knelt next to him as he struggled to gather them up. "Let me help."

"No, I cannot allow that. You are—"

"Yes, yes, high-born," I said. "Trust me, Pendragon, we're just boys, like you. Except we're not into this sort of thing."

Pendragon shook his head. "Your customs are strange. I fear I don't understand your words."

I sighed. "Okay, have it your way. We're high-born, but we're travelling incognito."

"I don't know where Cognito is, "Pendragon said. "Is it near Wynantskill?"

"We're in disguise, okay?"

"Yeah," Charlie said, as he helped me hold the bundle, "pretend we're just like you, and take us some place where there are other people."

"Your servant," he said, dipping his head as he looped twine around the sticks. It wasn't the sort of twine you'd buy at Wal-Mart, though. It was more like strips of leather. Whoever this kid was, he was deep into re-enacting, and we weren't part of the script. This gave me hope that he'd try to ditch us as soon as possible.

When the staves were secure, Pendragon lifted the bundle as if it were a bag of feathers and balanced it on his shoulder. Then he picked up the axe with his free hand and we followed him out of the clearing.

I rolled the cloak up, stuffed it under my arm and hurried to catch up. He led us along a path that ran beside an old stone wall nearly hidden beneath brambles and moss. He'd told us we were heading toward a road, but aside from the swishing of our feet in the tall grass and the light rustling of the leaves in the wind, there was no other sound. It gave me a strange and unsettling sensation, as if I was trudging through an alien landscape. The ancient stone wall told me that people used to be here, yet I got the feeling we were alone.

All around, as far as I could see, the land was empty, and lacking signs of civilization. Even the air seemed different. I breathed deep and sensed the unspoiled taste of the air in the Adirondack mountains, from the time Dad had taken us camping. I remembered the trip as cold, uncomfortable, and boring, but the air—far away from factories or highways packed with cars— was so pure and clear I felt like I could touch it. That's what I felt now, and I pondered again how impossible it would be for anyone to bring us here. But someone, somehow, must have, because there was no other way to explain what was happening. Then we came to the road.

I mentally high-fived myself, but then saw that it wasn't really a road. It was flat and wide enough for a car, but it was paved with stones and overdue for repairs. Weeds grew in the cracks between the rocks, and there were holes and cow plops—some old, some fresh—that we needed to avoid stepping in. It seemed dangerous to let someone walk on it, especially carrying a heavy load like Pendragon, but he stepped nimbly around the obstacles with practiced ease.

Charlie and I walked side by side behind him, scanning for anything that looked familiar. There were no buildings, cell towers or pylons in sight. Next to the road, the land was covered in trees and bushes that occasionally spilled so far over the roadway that we had to manoeuvre around them. We crossed an old, stone bridge over a sluggish creek and then I thought I saw a glint of white through the trees.

"What's that?" I asked Pendragon.

Pendragon stopped and looked to where I was pointing. Through a tangle of brambles, remnants of walls and a few broken columns were barely visible. Charlie and I squinted to see them better. Pendragon turned away and kept walking.

"That's where the giants lived," he said.

"Giants?"

Pendragon nodded but didn't look back. "They lived long ago. They built grand houses, and the road—this one, and many others, besides."

"So, where are they?" Charlie asked.

"Gone," Pendragon said. "No one knows when or why or how. They're just gone, and they left all this behind."

After that, his shyness left him and he began asking us questions, like, "How long have you been travelling," and "What places have you seen," and other sorts of questions you might ask a traveller in the

Middle Ages. I felt it was because he didn't want us asking any more questions about the giants, which I could understand. He was probably making it up as he went along. I let Charlie make up answers and kept scanning the landscape.

Once we passed the giant's house, the road began to deteriorate, and the freshness of the air took on a sour scent. The holes got larger and closer together and the smell stronger. Soon we were stumbling along a rutted dirt track and gagging from the stench.

"It smells like that farm we visited with Mom and Dad last year," Charlie said, wrinkling his nose.

I nodded. "Only worse."

Here, there were fewer trees and the land looked more used. Not that it was cultivated, it was simply less wild. Charlie tapped my shoulder and pointed. Ahead of us were houses. And people.

Chapter 8

The village, if that's what it was, looked like nothing I'd ever seen before. It was still some distance away, just beyond a sort of crossroad, where the muddy track we were on intersected with another muddy track running perpendicular to it. Houses clustered along what must have passed for the main street, most of them made of stone and all of them topped off with what looked like bundles of straw. Only a few people were on the road, all of them dressed in period costumes and carrying bundles or engaged in other middle-ages type activities. It wasn't what I'd hoped for, but it still made me optimistic. At least one of them should be willing to break out of character and help us.

Nearer to us, on our side of the crossroad, was a larger dwelling, also made of stone and topped with bundles of straw. It had an open yard in front, which was mostly churned up mud. Wooden rails and watering troughs lined the edges of the yard. Above the sturdy front door, a square piece of wood had been fastened to the stone. Painted on the wood was a picture of a green dragon.

"What's that house?" I asked Pendragon. There weren't many windows, and those that were there were small and narrow, but I thought I saw a light flickering in one of them. "Is there a phone in there?"

Pendragon shook his head and kept walking. "That

is the house of the brewer. It is not a place you should go into, even if you tell them who you are. It is a place where men drink. They would not welcome you."

Charlie went ahead of Pendragon and started walking toward the building. "But there are people in there, right?"

"Please, I beg you," Pendragon said, giving a good impression of sincere concern. "Our customs are different from yours. This you must not do."

"Listen, kid," Charlie said, "we've about had enough of this. You've led us to the town, so you can be on your way now. We'll take care of things from here. C'mon, Mitch."

I walked by Pendragon, who looked pitifully woeful. It was an astonishingly good act. "Thanks, Pendragon," I said, as I walked by. "Or whatever your real name is."

Charlie left the road and started picking his way across the yard, heading for the door of the big house. I followed, doing my best to keep the cloak from dragging in the mud.

Pendragon didn't follow, but he didn't leave us, either. "Sires, I beg you."

Then I heard another sound. A rhythmic thud, thud, thud coming from the road. I looked and saw a group of men on horseback, about a dozen in all, riding our way at a fast trot. Half of them wore tunics of red or blue with gold trim. The others—boys in their teens—were in less fancy clothes and rode behind the men. One of them held a long pole with a banner fluttering from it. On the banner was a picture of a red feather. The lead horse veered toward us, heading for the big house.

"There's some men on horses," I called to Charlie.

"I'll ask if any of them has a phone. You see if someone in that house can help us."

Charlie looked at the horses that were now entering the yard. He nodded at me, then pulled the door. It swung outward, revealing a dark interior. "Excuse me," he said, "can any of you— Whaa!"

Charlie dove aside as a wooden tankard sailed through the open doorway. It hit the ground and splashed liquid over the mud. Two men followed it out the door, both dressed in dull brown tunics. They had long hair and bushy beards and didn't look happy.

"Get back here, you whelp," they shouted, as Charlie dodged away from them and ran to me.

"What the—"

His words were cut short by the clatter of the horses, which were heading straight for us. The men stopped chasing Charlie and stood back. The horses trotted nearer, and I realized they weren't going to try to avoid us.

Then someone grabbed my arm and pulled. I struggled to keep upright, and saw Charlie, also being pulled. It was Pendragon. He'd put his bundle, and the axe, down at the side of the road and was now dragging us toward it. The horses trampled by. If he hadn't pulled us away, we'd have been stampeded over. None of the men on the horses even looked our way.

"That was well out of line," Charlie said. Then he shouted to the men. "What do you think—"

Pendragon shook him. "Shhhh!"

Charlie tried to pull his arm loose, but Pendragon held fast.

"Listen, buddy," Charlie said.

Pendragon, his face white, shook his head. "No, you listen. Forgive me, sires, but your customs put you in danger. If it is your intention to remain hidden, you must act like peasants. Peasants move away when knights ride by. If you don't, they will run you down."

Charlie laughed. "Knights? Where's their armour?"

Pendragon's brow furrowed. "Why would a knight wear armour if not in battle or at a tournament?"

The horses stopped near the doorway. The skinny man in the lead, with dark hair and a wispy beard, looked down at the men who had chased Charlie. "Hail," he said. "Who is master of this house?"

A voice boomed out, "Steric of Wessex." Then a stout man, wearing a leather jacket, canvas pants and floppy boots that came up to his knees, stepped into the doorway. He entered the yard and stood directly in front of the head knight. "Who hails me?"

"Looks like we got here just in time for the show," Charlie said.

The guy playing the head knight sat up straight. "Sir Fergus, knight of the king."

Beside me, Pendragon gave a low whistle. "I would be a knight, if I could." He kept his gaze on Fergus and finally let us go.

Steric put his fists on his hips and looked up at Fergus. "Your king holds no sway here, but hospitality knows no boundaries. Food and drink are within, come and rest."

Fergus shook his head. "I have no time for refreshment."

"Here it comes," Charlie said. "He's going to ask him to go on a quest."

"I and my brother knights are on a quest," Fergus said. "We seek brave men to accompany us."

Charlie laughed. "Got it in one."

"We would leave immediately for the forest in the

east to seek and kill the dragon that dwells within."

"Dragon," Charlie said. "That's such a cliché. Can't you do any better than that?"

"Please," Pendragon said, his eyes darting to Fergus for any sign he had heard, "keep your voice quiet. In this land, it is rude to interrupt a knight."

Charlie nodded. "Okay. I'll let them finish their little play."

"We have no quarrel with your dragon," Steric said.

Fergus leaned forward and gazed down at him. "Your courage fails you?"

"Courage we have plenty. Twelve years ago, the men of Horsham slew the dragon on the green." Steric paused and pointed to the sign over the doorway. "There is the name of my house, The Green Dragon. That shows our courage. It's desire we lack. There is no cause to stir up a dragon that gives us no trouble."

"No doubt poets will sing the praises of your caution," Fergus said. Then he looked around. By now, a few more men had gathered in the yard. "Is there no one of stout heart among you?"

"This is getting ridiculous," Charlie said. "Let's see if we can move it along."

He stepped away from us and approached the horsemen. "I'll kill your dragon" he said, in his best heroic cartoon voice. Beside me, Pendragon gasped.

The men, the knights, even Steric, looked shocked. Fergus turned his horse to face Charlie. "You mock me?"

I trotted to catch up with him, hoping Pendragon wouldn't follow and drag us away. "Sorry, sir," I said. "We didn't mean to interrupt, but we're lost, and we need to know the way home."

Fergus' face went red. "Sir Alwyn, flog these

insolent dogs."

A hefty man with broad shoulders, dismounted and came our way, holding something that looked like a medieval version of the little whips jockeys use to make their horses run faster, only his wasn't as small. He plodded toward us, his eyes narrow, his face set in a grimace showing yellowed teeth.

"Speak to a knight, will you?" he said, grabbing Charlie by the arm. "You'll learn manners."

"Hey!" Charlie said, struggling to pull free.

Alwyn raised the whip and I realized he was going to hit Charlie. He wasn't pretending. I dropped the cloak and lunged at him, grabbing his arm. It was solid as a baseball bat and just as unyielding. He was going to bring it down on both of us and there was nothing we could do to stop him. My head felt light as fear took over and everything crystallized: the rage on the man's face, his brown hair, tangled and falling to his shoulders, his brawny arm, mud splattered tunic and awful stench. The moment stretched out. I closed my eyes and waited for him to strike. But no blow came.

Then, the arm pulled away from my grasp. I opened my eyes. He had let go of Charlie and backed up a step, his face now pale. He stared at us, then turned to Fergus.

"My lord," he said. "These boys. They are soft as lambs."

"What concern is that to me? Strike them."

"They are clothed in strange attire and speak in an odd manner," Alwyn said, as he bent to pick up the cloak. "And they carry this."

"That's our blanket," I said.

Alwyn shook the cloak out and held it up, revealing the collar and the clasp.

"This is no blanket," he said. "It's a cloak."

Fergus stared, first at the cloak, then at us. "Who are you? And where did you come by this?"

"My name is Mitch, my brother is Charlie, and the cloak is ours," I said, my stomach still quivering. "Our grandfather gave it to us."

"Your grandfather? Is he a lord?"

I decided it was safer to play along. "Yes, he is."

"And he's rich," Charlie added.

Fergus nodded slowly. "I would see this cloak," he said.

Alwyn brought it to him. I wanted to object but kept quiet. I hoped Charlie would do the same.

"A fine cloak," Fergus said, as he inspected it. "A very expensive, and special, cloak." He looked at us. "You put yourselves in danger, travelling with such finery. In service to your Lord grandfather, I offer my protection. Travel with us. We will see to your safety, and to the safety of this cloak." I noticed he didn't say it was our cloak. I started to get a bad feeling.

I looked at Charlie. He furrowed his brow and shook his head.

"Swear fealty to me," Fergus said, a little more forcefully, "and I will see to your security."

"Thanks," I said, "but I think we'll just take our cloak and be on our way."

Fergus glared at me. "You refuse my hospitality?"

"I'm sorry," I said, "It's very generous of you, but it's not what we want. We just want our cloak."

I could see that Fergus didn't want to return it, and I mean, he didn't want to give it back, for real. Without all the witnesses, I think he would have stolen it, but instead, after glancing around and seeing all the people watching, he handed it back to Sir Alwyn.

"Thank you, good sir knights," I said, as I took the cloak from Alwyn and started backing away. Fergus continued to glare at us, and I got the feeling that, if he caught us alone, it wouldn't go well.

The tension broke when Steric clapped his hands. "My friends," he said. "Come, retire. Your horses need rest, as do you."

The knights looked to Fergus, who continued to watch us.

"We must wait for the baggage, sire," one of the others said. "And our horses need water."

Fergus nodded and they all dismounted, looking tired but cheered. The knights entered the house with Steric and a few of the men. The boys—who, Pendragon told us, weren't knights, but squires, a sort of knight in training—led the horses to the rails, tethered them with ropes and started removing the saddles as the horses drank from the troughs. The final knight to enter the house was Fergus, and he turned to look at us once more before he entered.

"What the hell was that all about," Charlie said, his voice still wobbly.

"I don't know, but at least we got our cloak back."

"Yeah, so now what?"

I shook my head. "We'll have to try in town. Those men aren't going to help us. In fact, I think we'd better steer clear of them."

"I did warn you." It was Pendragon, the bundle of sticks on his shoulder and the axe in his hand. "I would be a knight, but not like them. They lack honour. They wanted to steal your cloak." He ran his free hand over the thick material. "You were wise to call it a blanket. The worth of a garment such as this is beyond imagining. You are certainly lords."

"This is beyond ridiculous," Charlie said. "We need help, but no one seems to care."

"Come home with me," Pendragon said, almost pleading. "You can sup with us, and my father will know how to help you."

The idea of an authentic, re-enactment meal didn't sound appealing, but finally getting some help did.

"A one-on-one," I said, "with an adult."

Charlie nodded. "It's worth a try."

We followed Pendragon along the narrow track, away from the knights and the town. Charlie muttered about the re-enactors being idiots and how he was going to report them once we got home, but I thought about other things—what had just happened, what we had seen, where we were—and came to a conclusion that was as frightening as it was incredible.

"I don't think this kid is acting," I whispered to Charlie.

"You mean, he's just crazy?"

"No," I said. "I mean this isn't a re-enactment."

Chapter 9

"Think about it," I said, keeping my voice low. "A place like this, we'd have heard about it. And so close to our house? Don't you think we'd have come on a school trip? Or with Mom and Dad?"

Charlie plodded along next to me, his head down, watching his footing on the rutted track. "But that doesn't make it—"

"And did you see?" I asked, "Did you really look? Those men. They weren't wearing costumes. Their clothes were real. Filthy, smelly, and real. And the horses, their legs were spattered with mud, and they looked tired. They weren't just trotted out for our amusement. And that knight was really going to whip you."

"So, what does any of that prove?"

"It proves this isn't a re-enactment. And if it isn't a re-enactment, then it must be one of two other things."

"Which are?"

"A dream. Or this is actually real."

"So, a dream, then?"

I thought about it. "Yes, it would have to be, but it doesn't feel like a dream."

"Yeah," Charlie said, "dreams don't smell this bad."

"And they aren't this realistic. And did you hear what that man, Steric, said? He called this place Horsham. That's where Granddad lives."

"Well, that just proves this is a dream. How else could he know?"

"I suppose," I said. "Then it has to be a really weird dream. Maybe getting my head knocked put me in a coma. Maybe I'll never wake up."

Charlie stopped, put his hands on his hips and looked around at the fields and trees. "What about me? This is my dream."

I shoved the cloak under my arm and stepped toward him. "Then why don't you wake yourself up?"

"I guess I—"

I punched him in the chest.

"Oof! Hey, what was that for."

"Shouldn't that wake you up?"

Then I staggered sideways as Charlie punched me in the arm.

"Ow!"

"Did that wake you up?"

"Are my lords … well?"

Pendragon had stopped and was looking our way.

"Sorry," I said, rubbing my arm. "We're just deciding if this is a dream or not."

Pendragon nodded slowly. "I understand, my lords. If I were to travel to a far-off land, I would feel as if I were dreaming." He looked around. "But this is life. And all days are the same."

"Stop calling us lords," I said, "we're just Mitch and Charlie, okay?"

"As you wish, my … Mitch. Please follow. It is not far now." He turned and kept walking.

"Even if this is a dream," I said to Charlie as we continued following Pendragon, "don't do anything that's going to get us whipped. This dream hurts."

The path crossed another creek. The narrow bridge,

like the houses and the road into town, was made of stone, without the benefit of modern materials. On the far side, Pendragon left the road and led us on a path that ran alongside the creek. Here there were more fields, separated by tangles of brush and remnants of stone walls. There were also remains of buildings, square foundations lined up in a neat row, with weeds growing in the gaps. At the end of the row, a single building stood.

It was larger than the surrounding abandoned buildings, but only because a hodgepodge of extensions—most likely cobbled together with stones robbed from the neighbours—had been added. It, too, was covered in straw, and smoke seeped through the portion of it that covered the main hut. I wondered if it was on fire, but Pendragon didn't appear concerned. No weeds grew in front of it. The earth there was hard-packed, pocked with mud puddles and strewn with bits of wood and straw. A low stone wall, in need of repair, bordered the yard. Up against the far side stood a small structure made of rough boards where a few scrawny chickens scratched and pecked at the ground. Beyond the wall was a sort of fence made of sticks, woven together with more sticks. The fence was in need of repair too. Part of it lay in a broken heap on the ground next to a small cow, grazing on tufts of grass and tied to a stake.

Pendragon led us into the yard through a gap in the wall. He dropped his load of sticks next to the far wall and laid his axe on top of a large chopping block.

"I'll get fuel for the fire," Pendragon said, picking up hunks of wood from the jumbled pile next to the block, "then I will take you to mother."

But before he finished, the door of the hut, which

wasn't a real door but more of a woven mat hanging over the opening, moved aside and a woman came out. She was short, with long red hair and a weathered face. She wore a dress that looked like Pendragon's shirt, but longer, so that the hem brushed the ground, making it as dirty as her bare feet. She looked at Pendragon, then us, and smiled uncertainly.

"There you are, Pendragon," she said. "Who are your friends?"

Pendragon, clutching an armload of wood, stepped toward her, and encouraged us to do the same. "This is Mitch and Charlie," he said. "From the kingdom of Wynantskill. They are lost and require food and rest."

The woman came toward us and made a small curtsy. "I am Aisley, mistress of this house. You are most welcome."

"Welcome, indeed," came a gruff voice from beyond the house. "As if we have enough provisions to feed every beggar who comes this way!"

A great bear of a man entered the yard. He was only slightly taller than Aisley, but broad in the shoulders, with a black tangle of a beard that merged into his straggly hair, making his eyes the only thing you could see of his face. He wore a sleeveless shirt and loose pants made from a thick material, and on his feet were worn leather boots that came up to his knees.

"Garberend," Aisley said, "these boys are from a distant land. They are our guests."

"I think they might be nobles in disguise," Pendragon said quietly to his father.

"Nobles, eh?" Garberend asked. "You do not look noble to me."

"But, their hands," Pendragon said, "look at them, and the way they dress. And they have a cloak."

Garberend grabbed my free hand and ran his roughened fingers over my palm. "You are poorly acquainted with toil," he said. "But soft hands do not a nobleman make." Then he pulled the cloak from under my arm and held it high, letting it unfurl. "And this impressive, yet ill-fitting, garment." He looked down at me, his dark eyes narrow. "Do not think to lie to me. Did you come by it honestly?"

"Yes, sir," I said. "Our grandfather gave it to us. For our travels."

Garberend laughed. "Then you are surely not nobles. For no one of noble birth would call me sir." He rolled the cloak into a bundle and handed it back. "Your attire and demeanour speak more of troubadours than travelling nobles." He grabbed my arm and painfully massaged my bicep. "But whatever your station, you are in want of a good feed." Then he bowed low and swept his arm toward the entrance to the house. "Come then, young travellers, whoever you are, and sit at our table. Food and rest await within."

It was hard to tell with his face covered in hair, but I was pretty sure Garberend was smirking.

Chapter 10

We followed Aisley into the house while Garberend held the mat aside for us. The interior was dim and smoky, but neither Pendragon, nor his parents, took notice of it, or the pungent animal smell. I blinked away tears, waiting for my eyes to adjust to the gloom. Beside me, Charlie stifled a cough.

Pendragon dropped his load of wood next to a fire burning in the middle of the room, which was the source of the smoke. An iron frame arched over the fire and from it a black pot, shaped like a small cauldron, hung on a chain. Light filtered in through two small windows, lighting the room enough to reveal a few shelves, a small table, and a wooden washtub. The shelves and table were covered in earthenware jars, and clusters of vegetables, bound with twine, dangled from the beams crossing overhead. Otherwise, the room looked empty.

"Come, young lords," Garberend said.

He took the cloak from me and hung it on a peg, then he led us to the back of the room where, hidden in the dim light, was an immense table. He sat us on a bench near the back wall so we could see the room in front of us. Pendragon sat on the other side and Garberend sat on a three-legged stool at one end.

I ran my hand over the tabletop. It was solid oak, smooth and well crafted, and looked out of place when compared to the rest of the room. Its surface, though scarred and stained from years of use, showed no tool marks, and was marred only by some markings along one edge where something had been fastened to it.

"The young lord wonders at our table," Garberend said, looking my way. "Tell me, how does a poor farmer come by such a grand board?"

I felt he was expecting an answer. Maybe this was how he amused himself, quizzing his guests. He was obviously proud of the table, but how did he get it? I looked closer, trying to interpret the marks.

"Perhaps you need more light," he said, when I didn't answer.

As soon as he spoke, Aisley stopped tending the pot and brought over a clay bowl with some sort of liquid in it. There was a piece of cloth sticking up in the middle and she lit it with a stick from the fire. It sputtered and spit and smoked but the flame threw enough light for us to see more clearly.

"It was the door," Charlie said.

Garberend slapped his hand on the table and laughed. "Well played, young lord."

I looked again at the marks. Hinges, of course. And across the table, in front of Pendragon, were other marks that might have been for a latch. That was why they used a mat to cover the doorway.

"A waste of wood," Garberend continued. "Anything can keep out the cold, but only a king eats from a table as fine as this." He looked at us. "Or lords."

Aisley came again, carrying the pot, using a rag as a potholder, and set it on a charred slab of wood in the centre of the table. Garberend might not mind the occasional scratch, but he didn't want to burn a hole in his prize possession. "Stop teasing the boys," she said, "they came to us for help."

"And how could one such as I be of assistance?"

Aisley brought wooden bowls and spoons, and a board with a flat loaf of bread on it.

"They are lost," Pendragon said. "They need help finding their way home."

"From where do you hail?" Garberend asked, as Aisley poured frothy liquid into cups and set them in front of us.

"Wynantskill," I said.

At last, Aisley took her seat at the opposite end of the table. Then Garberend grabbed the bread, ripped it apart and the meal began. The main, and only, course was some sort of thick soup or thin stew, ladled out for us by Aisley, accompanied by the bread, which was coarse and tough. Even so, it tasted all right, except for the drink, which was like something I had never tasted before and didn't want to taste again. Charlie, too, made a face when he tasted it and set his cup back down.

"Are you not enjoying your beer?" Garberend asked.

"Beer?" I sniffed the cup and wrinkled my nose. "We're not allowed to drink beer."

"Then what do you drink?"

"Soda," I said, "or lemonade, or milk."

Garberend laughed. "Such strange customs. Come now, I have told you my tale of the table, tell me your tales of Wynantskill, where they drink no beer. What else do they forbid?"

"Well, for one thing," Charlie said, "we couldn't have an open fire in the middle of the room."

"Then how do you cook or heat your homes?"

"We cook in an oven," Charlie said.

"And if we did have a fire inside," I added, "we'd have it in a fireplace, with a chimney."

"Chimney?"

"You know, an enclosure, made of brick, or stones, to put the fire in, and a sort of tunnel to let the smoke out through the roof."

"That would let the heat out," Garberend said, "and the rain in."

"No, you'd just—"

"And the smoke," he continued, drawing a deep breath. I marvelled that he didn't choke. "It's good for you."

I wondered what era we were supposed to be in. If there were knights, it must be sometime in the Middle Ages. But surely they'd be more advanced than this, even in a dream.

"Your Wynantskill," Garberend said through a mouthful of bread, "it is far from here?"

"I think so," I said.

Garberend shook his head. "If you travelled to here from there, then surely you know. Was it days, weeks? Did you walk? Or did you ride horses?"

"Horses?" Charlie said. "We don't use horses."

Garberend shovelled up another spoonful of stew. "I wonder that you wish to return to this Wynantskill, where everything is forbidden."

"Horses aren't forbidden," I said. "We just don't need them. We have cars, carriages that move by themselves."

Garberend threw back his head and laughed. "Ah, that's more like it. What other tales can you tell?"

I looked at Charlie. "Why not?" he said. "It's just a dream."

So, we took turns eating and talking, telling them about refrigerators, microwave ovens, television, cell phones and the like, and after each story Garberend laughed and asked for more.

When we finished the meal, Garberend pushed his bowl aside and leaned toward us. "You weave words with great skill and your stories have more than earned your place at my table, but now I must return to my labours, and you to yours." Then he leaned back and chuckled. "Carts that move themselves. Next you'll tell me you can fly."

"Um, yeah, we can," I said. "Not in cars, but we have bigger carriages that hold lots of people, and they fly."

Garberend laughed again and wiped his eyes with the back of his hand. "You must show me. I would see this carriage that rides in the air."

"Well, I could draw one," I said. But when I looked around there wasn't a pencil or pad of paper to be seen.

"Do, I beg you," Garberend said. He pulled a knife from his belt, one with a metal blade. "Mark it here, on the table for me to see."

"But … I don't want to mar your fine table."

Garberend held the knife out, offering its handle. "It would honour me to see your flying carriage at every meal."

I went to where Garberend was sitting and took the knife. Being careful to not cut too deeply, I scratched a rough outline of an airplane in the tabletop around a large knot in the wood. By the time I finished, both Aisley and Pendragon were also watching.

"It is too dim to see," Garberend said taking the knife. Then he cut into the wood, following my tentative lines, digging deep. When he finished, I saw that he had squared off the curves. The result looked more like a cross with a black disk in the centre than an airplane, but I nodded and told him that was what they looked like.

"The people sit here," I said, tracing the fuselage, "the driver is up front, and these are the wings."

"And they flap, like a bird?" Garberend asked, waving his arms up and down.

"No," I said. "They're stiff. It glides in the air."

Garberend nodded. "Like a hawk hunting for prey."

"Yeah, sorta."

"What a grand story," Garberend said, sheathing his knife. "Your kingdom sounds a desirable place, despite the absence of beer and horses. But I fear I cannot help you find your way back, for I know of no such land."

I returned to my seat, feeling suddenly fatigued. I was tired of the whole "can you help us get home" thing. If this was a dream, there was no point. But if it was a dream, how come the smells, the sights, the sounds, and the tastes were all so vivid? I decided it didn't matter; I had to be dreaming.

"It's not that simple," Charlie said. "We were brought here."

I nodded and looked at Pendragon. "That's right. Tell him, Pendragon. Tell him how you found us, or how we found you."

"They came to me in the wood," Pendragon said, "as if they just appeared."

"We did," Charlie said. "We were in Wynantskill, and then we were here."

"They speak true, father."

Garberend rubbed a hand over Pendragon's head, mussing up his hair. "They have you well and truly beguiled, my son."

Then Aisley asked, "What brought you?"

"Dunno," Charlie said, as the room suddenly went silent. "Bobby knocked our heads together, I blacked out, and when I woke up, we were here. No reason. It just happened."

"No," I said, turning to Charlie. "It was the cloak. Don't you remember? Granddad said it was magic."

Pendragon jumped to his feet. "If the cloak brought you here," Pendragon said, "we can use it to take you home."

I shook my head. "We don't know how it works."

"Surely your grandfather told you how to harness its magic," Garberend said. I thought he was trying to be helpful, but he seemed to think we were telling another fable.

Charlie laughed. "He didn't send a user manual along with it."

I put my hand in my pocket. "Yes, he did," I said, pulling out the scroll. "This came with the cloak. Maybe it will give us a clue." I unrolled it and leaned toward the sputtering flame. It was difficult to see in the dim light, and the writing was spindly and hard to decipher, but soon it began to make sense.

"This transmigrating robe will send
Its wearer there and back again
By taking Morpheus' hand
You'll find a true and far-off land
And there a distant kin will show
Adventures waiting long ago."

I stopped, though there was still more to read. A lump of ice grew in my stomach, and I began to shake. I looked again at the writing, now clear and legible.

"You know your letters?" Garberend asked. He sounded amazed, as if I had just made a pig disappear or something.

"Of course," Charlie said.

I handed the scroll to him. "Read the rest," I said, pointing to where I had left off.

"Why don't you?"

"Just read it."

"It's all flowery, and I—"

"Just read it."

Charlie harrumphed and glared at the scroll.

"But traveller mark your entrance well
Or there forever you will dwell
For through that place, that place alone
You'll find the path to bring you home."

"There's your answer," Aisley said. "You need to go back to where you appeared."

"I can take you," Pendragon said.

"You should leave straight away," Garberend said. "Brighid will not linger long." He put a hand on Pendragon's shoulder. "And you have a paddock to repair before sundown."

I barely heard. My mind was still reeling.

Pendragon ran to get the cloak. Garberend rose and Aisley began clearing the table.

"Come on, Mitch," Charlie said as he stood up. "We might as well try. Maybe that will help us end this dream."

I looked up at him. When he saw my face, he sat back down.

"What's wrong?"

I held up the scroll so he could see it. "This isn't a dream."

Chapter 11

"What do you mean?" Charlie asked.

I pointed at the scroll. "You can't read in dreams."

Charlie shook his head. "That's nonsense. Of course you can."

"No. It was in a book, and it said if you were in a dream that was so vivid you couldn't tell it from real life, the thing to do was try to read something. In a dream, the words all smoosh together. I've tried it. But this ..." I held the scroll closer. "The words are clear. This is real."

"Maybe you're just dreaming you can read it, or I am."

"Are you ready, my lords?" It was Pendragon, standing by the fire, holding our cloak.

Charlie nodded and got up. "Dream or not, we're going back to where we started. That's what it said to do. Maybe the dream-logic will put things right."

"We need to be careful," I said. "That knight ..." A chill tightened around my stomach at the memory. "... he was going to whip us."

"Okay," Charlie said, moving away, "we'll stay away from trouble if it makes you feel better."

I followed and we all left, returning to the fresher air in the farmyard.

Garberend slapped me on the back, nearly knocking me sideways, and thanked us for our company and our stories. He then told Pendragon to get more staves and to bring the withies back so he could fix the fence before nightfall. The sky was still cloudy, but it felt like midday or just after. Pendragon had a lot of work to do, and he seemed anxious to get us moving. He was practically jumping with excitement at having an adventure.

Garberend left, walking into the fields behind the house. I took the cloak from Pendragon, who reluctantly gave it up. He and Charlie started walking, expecting me to follow, but Aisley came to me and rested a hand on my shoulder.

"My husband is a good man," she said, stooping to my level, "but he lives in this world, and imagines no others."

"What do you mean?"

"You are not mere storytellers," she said. It was a statement, not a question. "My son speaks true. You appeared, just as he says." I hugged the cloak to my chest, unsure how to respond. Her hand left my shoulder and tentatively touched the velvet material. "The cloak brought you, but it is the gods who sent you."

"What ... are you saying you believe us?"

She nodded slowly. "Their power is great," she continued, "but they do not use it lightly. You are here for a reason."

I looked toward the path, where Charlie and Pendragon were waiting for me. "Maybe," I said, "but they didn't tell us what it is, so we're going home now."

She gazed at me for a few moments, neither agreeing nor disagreeing. Then she said, "The gods have set a path for you. You can choose to walk it, or you can walk your own. Choose wisely."

She stepped away then, and waved to Pendragon and Charlie as I hurried to catch up with them.

"What was that all about?" Charlie asked.

"Nothing," I said, not wanting to admit how spooked it had made me. "She just wanted to see the cloak."

"What for?"

"It's magic," Pendragon said. "Who wouldn't want to see it?"

A thought came to me. I froze, not wanting to take another step forward. "The knights," I said.

Pendragon and Charlie both stopped and turned.

"What about them?" Charlie asked.

"They might still be at The Green Dragon. That guy, Fergus, he'll try to steal the cloak if he sees us." I turned to Pendragon. "Is there another way back to where we were? One that doesn't go past there?"

Pendragon nodded. "It is longer and will take more time, but I think you may be right. Those knights were not honourable. We should avoid them if we can."

He started back the way we came, and we fell into step behind him.

"We can go through the marketplace, to the north road. There is a path that will take us around the village."

"Do you really think this is necessary?" Charlie asked.

"Yes. We need to avoid any trouble or we're not going to make it home."

"This is my dream, you know. I could make you do what I want."

I kept walking. "But you won't."

We passed Pendragon's home and continued to a rickety footbridge across the creek. From there, a path

62

led us past a stone building, larger and more impressive than the houses we had seen.

"It's a temple," Pendragon said, when I asked about it. "To our gods."

"Gods?" Charlie asked. "You have more than one?"

Pendragon, still walking, recited a list of names that meant nothing to me. The only ones of note were Brighid, who Garberend had mentioned, and the final one, who he called "the God-man, Christ."

I looked at Charlie, but he shook his head, and we didn't ask any more.

Beyond the temple were more houses, larger and better built than the others we had seen. They were spaced along a narrow street running from the temple to an open area that might have, at one time, been a field but was now just an expanse of mud. It was dotted with ramshackle carts and booths, all piled with vegetables, or slabs of meat, oozing blood and buzzing with flies. A dozen or so people milled around and the tangy scent of wood smoke—mingled with the stench of animals—filled the air. A woman emerged from a nearby house hauling a wooden bucket slopping brown sludge as it bumped against her thigh. She carried the bucket to the road, dumped its contents into the mud and returned to the house. Ahead of us, a man drove half a dozen small pigs between the carts.

We kept walking, trying to remain inconspicuous, which wasn't easy dressed the way we were.

"Pendragon," a woman called. "Are they your strange friends?"

"Where are they from?" called another.

"Did they come with the knights?" asked a man as he shooed a pig away from his cart.

"They are travellers," Pendragon said. "From far

away, further than the knights."

"So young?"

"How did they get here?"

"We would hear their story."

"We are in haste," Pendragon said. Then he turned to us and whispered, "News travels fast through the village. We may be long delayed if we tarry."

Charlie and I glanced at the curious stares of the villagers. "You're right," Charlie said. "Let's go."

We walked on, and nearly bumped into an old man wearing a shabby cloak. He was stooped, with straggly black hair and a thin beard. He held his filthy cloak tightly around his lean body as if to ward off a chill.

"Watch out for him," a woman called out. "He'll steal your eye teeth and then try to sell 'em back to you."

I took a step back and held the cloak tight to my chest.

"Come now," the man said, limping forward. "She jests. I am a traveller, like yourselves, and a teller of tales."

"Tales?" Charlie asked.

"We need to be on our way," I said.

"But surely you would hear of the great dragon that inhabits the forest in the east. That terrible lizard, that cunning adder, that wicked snake. Oh, I could tell you many tales about him."

"Everyone knows about the dragon," Pendragon said. "And we are in haste."

Pendragon tried to move around him, but the man blocked his path by side-stepping in front of him. He moved quickly for an old man with a limp.

"Ah, you know of the dragon," he said, looking from Pendragon to Charlie and then to me. "But your friends, they are from far away, what do they know? Are they aware of the danger they face?"

"Enough," Pendragon said. "Let us pass."

The old man's thin lips turned up into a sly smile. "Do you know the tale of the dragon? How he overcame a poor young woman from this very village."

"Really?" Charlie said.

"Oh yes! Took her, he did. And then …"

He leaned closer.

"And then what?" Charlie asked.

The man's smile widened, then he recited:

"I should howl outright to tell the rest,

How this poor maiden was over pressed.

Therefore come, and hear, for your penny!

Come, my hearts! 'Tis as good a tale as any.

There's no Sussex Serpent to frighten you here,

But a penny apiece will put it in your ear."

He stopped then and gazed at us expectantly. I leaned toward Pendragon. "What does he mean by that?"

"If you want to hear the story," Pendragon said, "we have to pay him."

"Pay to hear a story?" Charlie asked.

The man gave a small bow. "Unless you know of another way for an honest traveller like myself to earn his bread."

"Well, we don't have any money," I said, "and we don't want to hear your story, so we'll just be on our way."

The man shook his head and wagged a grubby finger at us. "No money? Finely dressed lads like you, with such an exquisite cloak. Now who is telling tales?" He reached for the cloak. "Such a garment would be worth a tale or two, if you wished to trade it for mine."

I pulled back and Pendragon stepped between me and the old man to protect the cloak. "No," he said, "we're not trading, we are leaving."

"We'd better go," said Charlie. "Now!"

We moved around the man and walked as quickly as we could, but I had barely enough time to wonder how he knew the bundle I was carrying was a cloak, when I was pushed from behind.

The man, no longer a stooped, old man, shoved me into Charlie, and Charlie into Pendragon, and we all fell into the fetid mud. Before I could get up, the man wrenched the cloak from my grip and ran.

"He's got the cloak," I shouted as we struggled out of the sludge. "After him!"

We ran as fast as we could, but the thief was far ahead of us, his cloak flapping behind him like a cape, our cloak tucked securely under his arm.

"Stop! Thief!" Pendragon shouted.

Some of the people tried to grab the fleeing man, but he dodged around them, slipped between the carts and booths, and ran on. A few villagers joined the chase and by the time we reached the edge of the village, a dozen men and women were in pursuit.

I struggled along with Charlie, following Pendragon and the villagers, pumping my legs, pushing hard, until my sides ached and my thighs felt like rubber. Far ahead of us, the thief ran like a rabbit. We had no chance of catching him, but we had to try. We needed to get the cloak back.

We slowed to a jog, gasping and shouting, while the thief loped far ahead of us and the pursuing mob.

I leaned over, my hands on my knees, panting hard. "We're never going to catch him."

"There are others in pursuit," Pendragon said,

showing no signs of fatigue. "Follow them."

Charlie leaned against a tree, sucking in huge gulps of air. "He's right. As long as … we don't lose them … there's still hope."

We'd left the village on a wide path that had quickly narrowed and then disappeared as the grass and shrubs gave way to trees. Soon, the woods thickened, and the pursuers lost enthusiasm. Some gave up and began walking back toward town. Even Pendragon slowed his pace.

"We can't go into the forest," he said, "there's a dragon."

"Forget the dragon," I said. "We need the cloak."

Fear of losing the cloak blocked out everything else. Charlie and I ran deeper into the trees with Pendragon reluctantly following.

"I have never been in this wood," Pendragon said. "I won't know my way out"

I kept running. "The people we're following, they'll know."

Pendragon didn't object, even though he probably knew what I suspected: that the people chasing the thief hadn't been this deep into the forest either, not if they believed the stories about the dragon. Even if we did get our cloak back, we might not be able to get back to the village. I put the thought out of my mind. One problem at a time.

The villagers were so far ahead we could no longer see them. We had to stop occasionally to listen for their shouts and then run toward them, heading deeper into the forest, struggling to keep up as the trees became thicker and the light dimmer. No matter how fast we ran, the shouting became more and more distant and difficult to follow. It seemed to be coming from everywhere, causing us to run in one direction, then another. None of us were sure which way we were going but we were pretty certain we weren't heading back toward the village. We'd been in pursuit for a while and had to be over a mile away from the village, and Pendragon was getting increasingly uneasy.

We stopped again, resting, listening, trying to stifle our breathing so we could hear.

There were no sounds of people running, no shouts, nothing.

"What do we do now?" Charlie asked, his voice wavering. "If they've lost him, or we've lost them, then we'll never get the cloak back."

"The cloak is not our only problem," Pendragon said. "I am not sure I can find the way back. We need to find the others."

I fought down my panic and listened again, more intently this time, hoping for a miracle. Something had to go right. Things couldn't get any worse than this.

A scream broke the stillness, and then another—long, horrified screams of people fearing for their lives.

Charlie pointed toward the sound. "This way."

We ran, blundering through bushes in our rush to find them, whoever it was.

The screams died away, leaving a terrifying silence behind. Seconds later, they came again, louder and closer, accompanied by the sound of pounding feet. The few remaining villagers still in pursuit were now retreating, dodging through the trees, running toward us, their faces white and their eyes wide with fright.

"Run for your lives," they screamed.

The men bounded past us. We turned to follow, but then heard another sound. Someone else was coming toward us, pounding through the trees. More villagers?

But there was no shouting, just a low growl that turned into a roar. Charlie grabbed my arm and pointed into the forest. "Look."

Something was coming. Something big. And it was nearly upon us.

Pendragon tried to run but Charlie and I grabbed him and pulled him to the ground.

"Keep still," I said. "If we run, whoever it is will see us."

Then, through the trees, I spotted a large, leathery head with a pointed snout and eyes that glowed like burning coals. The head, with smoke billowing from its nostrils, looked left and right and gave another roar. Pendragon shook so hard I thought he might pass out.

Charlie sank lower, trying to disappear into the forest floor. "What the hell?"

Beside me, still trembling, Pendragon said, "It's the dragon."

Chapter 12

The dragon roared again.

It took both of us to keep Pendragon from giving us away. Fortunately, he was weak with fear, but he kept panting and whining, "It's going to kill us, it's going to kill us."

"Not if you keep still and shut up," Charlie hissed.

I turned my head slowly and peered through the bushes. The dragon was thirty feet away, its head still swaying from side to side as if searching for prey.

"This has gotta be a dream," Charlie said. "Dragons aren't real." But I noticed he didn't stir from his hiding place.

"Perhaps in your land," Pendragon whimpered. "Here … look … your eyes do not deceive you."

The dragon began to move, but not in our direction. It seemed to be turning around to head back the way it came.

"Yes, they do," I said. Both Charlie and Pendragon looked at me. I pointed toward the dragon. "Look at it."

Charlie shuffled up next to me to get a look, and Pendragon, still white with fear, lay next to him. The dragon was now turned away from us. If it hadn't been, I'm sure Pendragon would have screamed and ran. As it was, he just shook his head and said, "It's the dragon, the dragon …"

"No," I said. "Really look at it. Use your eyes, not your imagination. Don't let your fear fool you."

The three of us watched as the dragon retreated deeper into the forest.

"It's got no legs," Charlie said.

It was true. The dragon's body was a series of uneven humps that moved in an ungainly fashion, dragging a strangely limp tail behind. The scales on its body, which appeared to be green strips of fabric, fluttered in the breeze.

Pendragon gradually stopped shaking. "It's ... it's not a dragon," he said. "It's a puppet."

"Yes," Charlie said. "There's men inside, making it move. It's fake."

"Exactly," I said. "I don't think that old man was a lone thief. There must be a whole band of them out here and they use the dragon to scare people off. That's why he was spreading stories about it."

"We need to tell the village," Pendragon said.

"We need to find out where it's going first," I said. "They have to have someplace to keep the dragon costume, and that many people will need a place to live."

Charlie shook his head and sighed. "You're not suggesting we follow it, are you?"

"We have to," I said. "He's got the cloak. We need to find them again once we get back to the village for help."

"But we might get lost," Charlie said.

"We're already lost," I reminded him. "We just have to keep from getting more lost. We'll mark our trail from this point."

"How?" Charlie asked.

Pendragon sat up. His colour had returned, and he

was no longer shaking. "I know," he said. "Keep an eye on the dragon."

We kept watch as the dragon moved through the trees. Meanwhile, Pendragon dug up a lump of rock. He then hit it with another rock, shaving a slice off, leaving him half a stone with a razor-sharp edge.

"It's almost out of sight," Charlie said.

Pendragon struck a nearby tree, cutting through the bark to leave a bright blaze of exposed wood. "Okay," he said. "Let's go. But keep out of sight and move silently."

Pendragon, now fully recovered, proved better at that than we did. He moved swiftly and without a sound and soon we took to following him at a distance so we wouldn't give ourselves away, while Pendragon kept the men in the dragon costume in sight and cut a mark every ten yards or so.

We kept going until Pendragon stopped and laid behind a bush. We joined him and watched as the dragon disappeared over a rise, then we moved forward. Beyond the rise was a wide basin with a scattering of trees and bushes, and beyond that a rocky hill. It was steep, more of a cliff, with the bottom half hidden behind a tangled mass of bushes. As the dragon drew near, a section of the brush opened and a half dozen men emerged.

Then the dragon tilted sideways and another half dozen men slithered out from beneath it. One of them was the thief, still holding our cloak.

"We're safe enough now," the thief, who appeared to be in charge, said. "Open up the camp."

The man who had been operating the dragon's head pulled out a small cauldron of smoking embers, which had helped us imagine the dragon's fiery breath. It was on some sort of metal framework and, once it was out, the dragon's leather head collapsed and the other men rolled it up, along with the body and tail.

Two of the men pulled the dragon costume through the doorway, others lifted what looked like blankets of leaves, exposing two windows, and another one pulled a bush aside, revealing an open pit. The man carrying the smoking embers dumped them into the pit and began building a fire. Some of the men sat next to it. Two others walked away, into the forest, and one of them headed our way.

"They must be lookouts," Pendragon said. "We need to go."

We followed the marks back to where we had originally seen the dragon and scanned the forest. Then Charlie and I looked expectantly at Pendragon.

"Okay," Charlie said. "Now how do we get back to the village?"

Pendragon looked around. "I don't know. I've never been in these woods. There's—"

"A dragon," Charlie said. "I know. But you still must have some idea where you are."

Pendragon pointed. "Well, I do know we came from that way," he said, but his voice lacked conviction.

We moved on, led by hope and an occasional footprint or broken branch left by the fleeing men. It was slow going. The sky remained overcast, and the woods closed around us, giving us no clue as to what direction we were heading in. Now that the excitement was over, boredom settled in, and I began to feel the chill in the air. I rubbed my arms in an attempt to keep warm, following behind Pendragon, who continued marking trees so we could lead the villagers back. If we got to the village. After an hour or two, the footprints disappeared, and our hope began to wane.

"If we don't find our way out soon," Pendragon said, "we will have to spend the night."

I stopped, feeling the first tendrils of panic gripping my chest. "What?"

"Brighid has nearly finished her journey. It will be dark soon."

"Well, we'll just have to keep going until then."

Pendragon shook his head and plodded forward. It was clear that the sun, wherever it was, was setting. The dim light of the forest was getting dimmer, and it wouldn't be long before it got dark. We were far from home, cold, tired, and hungry. I felt the tendrils tighten around me.

"Hey," Charlie said, pointing into the woods. "There's a mark on that tree over there."

We went to look at it. When he saw it, Pendragon sat down hard, as if the will to live had deserted him. "That's a mark I made," he said. "We are going in circles."

I slumped down next to him, feeling the same way I imagined he did. "What do we do now?"

Charlie sat next to me. No one said anything for a while. Except for the rising panic, my mind was empty. I hated to admit it, but I was counting on Pendragon to pull us through. Fortunately, he didn't disappoint.

"We'll have to make camp," he said, "and wait for morning."

It wasn't what I wanted to hear, but I knew he was right; there was nothing else we could do. We all got up, and Charlie and I began following Pendragon's orders—collecting sticks, breaking off small branches, pulling vines off trees—while he fashioned a crude lean-to under a big tree. When the lean-to was complete, we heaped leaves and pine needles under it to make a dry, leafy mat to sleep on.

When we finished, we sat down inside it. There wasn't much room, and it didn't really keep us much warmer.

"What we need now is a campfire," Charlie said.

Pendragon looked up, his face hopeful. "Do you have a striking iron and tinder?"

"Well, no," Charlie said. "I was kinda hoping you'd bang some rocks together or something."

Pendragon sighed. "Is that how you bring fire in Wynantskill?"

"No," I said. "We have central heating, and electric lights."

Pendragon didn't respond. I think he was getting tired of our stories. We sat in silence watching the night creep in.

"It will be a cold night," Pendragon said when it was nearly full dark. "We should sleep close."

We arranged ourselves on the makeshift mat, Charlie near the back, then Pendragon, then me, the three of us pressed together for warmth. Being on the outside meant that only one side of me could be warm, and I soon found myself shivering slightly and wondering if Charlie was warmer for being toward the back of the lean-to.

"Without a fire," Pendragon said, "you are going to be very cold."

"That's okay," I said. "It's my own fault for dressing in summer clothes for a trip in … what month is this, anyway?"

"We are in the summer cycle, a moon before the harvest."

"Summer!" Charlie said. "I'd hate to see winter."

We tried to settle down. I turned to face into the forest so I could warm my back. It was amazing how black it was. Until then, I had never believed the saying "too dark to see your hand in front of your face," but now, I waved my fingers in front of my eyes, and saw nothing.

"What are you doing?" Pendragon asked.

"I'm just ... I can't believe it's this dark."

"Yeah," Charlie said. "It's like that time I went to Howe Caverns on a school trip, and they turned the lights off for a few minutes to show us what dark really looked like."

"You don't have dark where you come from?" Pendragon asked. "Have you harnessed Brighid?"

"Sure, we have dark," Charlie said. "But we also have lights, portable fire, that you can carry around with you to keep the dark away."

"Like torches?"

"Yes, but you don't need to bang rocks together to light them. You just have to push a button."

"Who is this Brighid you keep talking about?" I asked when the silence returned.

She is our most powerful goddess," Pendragon said. "She protects the land. She lights the day."

"So, she's the sun?" Charlie asked.

"No," Pendragon said. "She controls the sun, and the moon. And like the sun and the moon, she has two faces—a beautiful, light one, and an ugly dark one."

"So, she's like night and day," I said.

Pendragon paused, then said. "In a way. She imparts wisdom, or she may try to trick you. That's all I know. That's all I need to know."

I had more questions, but none of us really felt like

talking. I hugged myself against the cold, turned away from the forest and tried to sleep, hoping that, if this was a dream, I'd be back home when I woke up.

I struggled to sleep, but at some point, fatigue must have taken over because I dreamed I was warm, lying next to a roaring fire. Then, slowly, I realized I wasn't dreaming. I was really being warmed by a real fire. I heard the snap and crackle of burning wood and smelled smoke. The forest must be on fire.

I sat up quickly, banged my head on the lean-to and knocked it over. Pendragon and Charlie thrashed, trying to push the branches away. I looked around. The forest wasn't burning, but a few feet away, in a circle of cleared ground, flames from a campfire flickered high into the night. On the far side of the fire, nearly hidden by the flames, sat a man wearing a robe.

I shook my head, trying to clear my thoughts. I had to be dreaming. First a dragon, now a wizard.

Pendragon sat up next to me. "What—" Then he started shaking again. He pointed at the man. "A Druid. Run. They eat children."

Chapter 13

Charlie thrashed, throwing sticks and leaves aside. "What the ... who lit the fire?"

"Druid," Pendragon shouted again. He climbed to his feet and tried to pull us up. "Run. Quick."

I looked at the man by the fire. He hadn't made a move toward us. In fact, he hadn't made a move at all. His face was hidden in shadow under the robe's hood and all I could see were his hands, which lay in his lap, holding a long stick. For a moment I thought he wasn't real, that he was just another puppet, like the dragon, but then he raised a hand.

"Mitch, Charlie," he said, "tell your friend Pendragon he has nothing to fear."

"He knows our names," Charlie said.

"He's trying to beguile us," Pendragon said, though he at least stopped pulling on my arm.

"If I had wanted to eat you," the Druid said, "I would be feasting by now. Come. Sit by the fire and warm yourselves."

Pendragon didn't move. Charlie inched forward. "Who are you? What's going on?"

The Druid laughed. "Always wanting to know everything at once, instead of letting the mystery resolve itself." He gestured to the fire. "Come. We need to talk."

Slowly, I got to my feet and walked to the fire.

"How do you know us."

"I have met you before."

I sat down. Charlie and Pendragon sat beside me.

"I don't think so," Charlie said. "I'd have remembered."

"I didn't say you have met me, only that I have met you. It was long ago, when you are older."

Charlie looked at me. "This has to be a dream because that doesn't make any sense."

"Do your dreams often leave you cold, hungry and thirsty?" the Druid asked, pulling a leather sack from behind him. He tossed it to Charlie who caught it awkwardly.

"Hey!" Charlie said. "What are you ... oh, thanks."

Inside the bag were hunks of bread and something that looked like cheese.

"Eat," the Druid said. He tossed a water skin to Pendragon. "And drink. I will wait."

We shared out the food. The bread was dry, and the cheese tasted like old socks, but I was too hungry to care. By the time we finished, the fire had warmed me, and I began to feel more normal. Or as normal as I could while being lost in a forest in medieval England talking to a Druid.

While we ate, the Druid sat silent, both hands resting on the stick. It wasn't the kind of stick you'd throw for your dog to fetch. It was long, like a walking stick, or a staff, gnarled and darkened with age. He didn't move at all, but when we finished, he leaned forward and the flames from the campfire lit his face. He had a grey beard and moustache, but mostly I saw his eyes, glowing in the light, a deep, sparkling blue, and around his right eye curled the white line of a scar.

"Why are you here?" he asked."

Charlie squeezed a final mouthful of water from the skin. "Shouldn't we be asking you that?"

The Druid chuckled and leaned back, his face once again obscured by shadow. "I know why I am here."

"We're looking for our cloak," Charlie said. "A thief stole it. We chased him. We got lost. End of story."

"That's why you're in this forest," the Druid said. "But why are you here?"

Charlie shook his head. "That doesn't make—"

"The gods," I said. "We were sent by the gods. They used the cloak to bring us here."

Both Charlie and Pendragon looked at me.

"What are you talking about?" Charlie asked.

"The gods?" Pendragon asked.

"It's what your mom said to me, while you were waiting. She said the gods brought us, and they had a plan. She didn't think we should try to go back home. She said they had a path for us to walk, and we shouldn't turn away from it, or something like that."

Pendragon's mouth fell open, Charlie threw his hands into the air. "And you didn't think to tell us?"

"I didn't want to make things worse."

Charlie looked around at the ruined lean-to and the forbidding forest. "Worse than what?"

"Your mother speaks wise, young Pendragon," the Druid said. "There is a path, and you are, indeed, on it. The question now is, what are you going to do about it?"

"We're going back to the village," Charlie said. "We'll find help. We'll get our cloak back."

The Druid nodded slowly. "A sound plan, if you can find the village, and if you return to the thief in time."

"They don't look like they're planning on going

anywhere," Charlie said.

"They are not," the Druid said. "But there are other forces at work. This is what I have come to tell you."

He leaned forward slightly, drawing our attention. "Your thief is Fyren, as clever as he is ruthless, with many who aid him. And many who wish to find him."

"You know the thief's name?" I asked.

The Druid nodded. "I do. He is part of your path, and you are part of his."

"So, if you know who he is," Charlie said, "and we know where he is, can't you put out an APB or something?"

"Finding Fyren is not the issue," the Druid said. "What matters is who finds him first."

None of us spoke. I didn't know about Charlie or Pendragon, but I was getting tired of playing the guessing game. The Druid, unfortunately, was not.

"Do you think it was merely bad luck that Fyren stole your cloak?" he asked. "He knew you were here, and he knew where to find you, and he desperately wanted your cloak."

"But we hardly know we're here," I said, "and we didn't decide to take that route until the last minute. How could he have known?"

"Because of another item he has stolen. Something more powerful than he can understand. A sacred amulet, called the Talisman."

Charlie looked at me. "First a cloak, now a talisman. You can't tell me this isn't a dream. What is the Talisman? A magic wand or something?"

The druid chuckled. "Always the doubter. But with a healthy, questioning mind."

We all looked at him. Even though we couldn't see his face I felt that he had become serious again.

"The Talisman is an ancient scrying stone, forged from Star Fire by the two-faced goddess, Brighid, and imbued with her power. The Talisman is from the Land, and it watches over the Land, but like Brighid, there is a light side and a dark side. It can be to the benefit of the Land, or to its detriment. In the hands of the honourable, the Land prospers, in the hands of those who seek their own gain, the Land withers.

"And the Talisman does not merely influence the Land. Those who possess it are also touched by its power. Look into the Talisman and, if your heart is true, you will find the ugly face of truth. This will be your curse. Look into the Talisman with a dark heart, and the beauty of empty promises will beguile you. This will be your downfall. Only a stalwart heart is strong enough to accept truth and follow it to the light. A dark heart will follow falsehoods to ruination. The heart the Talisman finds is the one you have chosen. Choose wisely."

He turned his head slightly when he said the final two words. I felt he was looking directly at me, and I heard them echo the words Aisley spoke.

"What's that got to do with us?" Charlie asked.

"Everything," the druid said. "The cloak you possess is not simply a magician's cape, something to conjure tricks with. The cloak ties you to the Talisman. Whoever rightfully possesses the cloak is the Guardian of the Talisman. Fyren knows this. This was why the Talisman told him where the cloak was, and why he had to steal it. He now considers himself the Guardian, and the rightful possessor of the Talisman."

"But it's not his cloak," I said. "It's ours."

"And that is why he will fail. You are the bearers of the cloak. You are the Guardians of the Talisman. You must take back what is yours, rescue the Talisman and return it to its rightful owner."

For a few moments, the snapping of the fire was the only sound. Then Charlie spoke. "You'll help us, right? Get back to the village, I mean, so we can raise a posse, and you can show us where this Talisman is?"

The Druid shook his head.

"But we need to go back to the village for help," I said. "Otherwise, we'll never get our cloak."

"This task is yours, alone."

I started to protest again, but the Druid raised his hand. "There are others who would possess the Talisman. They are not put off by danger. You must act before they do."

"They're welcome to the Talisman," Charlie said. "We just want our cloak back so we can get out of here."

The Druid said nothing, and I began to wonder if what Charlie said had made him angry, or convinced him that we weren't up to the task. But then he spoke, his voice soft but firm.

"The two are one. If anyone takes the Talisman, they will take the cloak, as well. This is what you must understand: Fyren stole the talisman, and the cloak. He does not possess them by right. Whoever liberates them from his grasp will be the rightful Guardian, and that Guardian can be wise and honest, or deceitful and foolish. It is your choice to decide who becomes the Guardian."

"Is this the path Aisley told me about?" I asked.

The Druid nodded. "It is."

"But we don't really have to do this," Charlie said. "We can decide to do something else, something sensible, like get help."

"You can," the Druid said, rising to his feet. He was tall, but his staff was taller than he was. "Rest your minds. Sleep warm by the fire. In the morning, your path will become clear."

He picked up a pack that had been lying behind him, gathered the food sack and water skin and slung the pack onto his shoulder.

"You're leaving us?" Charlie asked.

"Your task is here. Mine is on another path, but both are equally important."

I had just become accustomed to not feeling terrified, and now the fear gripped me again. "But how are we supposed to find the Talisman if we don't know what it is?"

"You will know the Talisman when you find your cloak."

He left us then, stepping out of the clearing and into the forest.

"Thanks for nothing!" Charlie shouted as he disappeared into the gloom.

"The answers are within you," the Druid said from the darkness. "By learning to find them yourselves, all knowledge will be open to you."

I looked at Charlie and Pendragon. "What was that all about?"

"A quest," Pendragon said, his eyes practically glowing with an excitement I didn't share.

"Are Druids always like that?" Charlie asked. "And do they really eat children?"

"I don't know," Pendragon said, still staring at the place where the Druid had been. "I've never seen a Druid. The legends say they are all dead."

"But that thing about eating children."

"The legends—"

"We're children," Charlie said. "And he didn't eat us, and he certainly had the chance. So maybe that part's wrong. And the part about them being dead."

Pendragon stared into the fire. "Yes. Perhaps the legends are wrong."

From the darkness, the Druid's voice came again, faint, but clear. "Now you are learning."

We gasped and looked around at the gloom just beyond the small circle of light thrown by the fire. The Druid's voice seemed to be coming from every direction.

"That guy is a fountain of useless information," Charlie said. "It'd be nice if he told us something helpful."

"Fyren's fortress has a flaw," the voice said, growing fainter. "Ask yourself how you can take advantage of it."

"What flaw?" Charlie shouted into the dark. "Tell us something useful."

We sat still, listening to the noises of the night, the crackling of the fire, waiting.

Then the voice came again, faint and distant. "Beware the Black Dragon."

Then the silence returned.

"Do you think he's gone now?" Charlie whispered.

"I think so," I said.

"What did he mean?" Pendragon asked.

"Who knows," I said. "But there's not much to be gain by sitting up all night thinking about it. We should sleep now."

Pendragon got up and began gathering sticks. "Help me build up the fire so it will last longer."

In the end, we threw the wreckage of the lean-to on it and made rough mats from leaves and settled down to sleep in the open.

"How can I sleep knowing he's out there?" Pendragon asked.

"If he was going to harm us," I said, "he would have. That makes me believe we can trust him. And you heard what he said, in the morning, we'll know what to do."

Charlie and Pendragon grumbled but said nothing. We were no longer hungry or thirsty, and we were warmer than we had been, but we were still lost. There was no use talking about it, though, so we just tried to sleep as best we could.

Chapter 14

I woke cold and stiff and disappointed. I was still in the forest, not in my own bed, or even in a hospital bed with tubes and wires attached to me. Disappointed, but not surprised. I think I was coming to accept the impossible.

Charlie, however, seemed to be struggling. He opened his eyes, looked around and slammed his fist into the dirt. "Damn."

I sat up. The light was dim, the air chilly and the forest filled with the sound of chirping birds. Pendragon was kneeling by the ashes that used to be a fire, laying small sticks on the coals and blowing on them. A tendril of smoke rose, followed by a flame, and soon, the fire was large enough to warm us again. Mist still lingered in the forest, however, so I knew we were going to be cold again soon. We couldn't take the fire with us, and we couldn't huddle around it all day.

We sat for a while, not talking, warming our hands, our backs, our feet, avoiding the question none of us wanted answered.

Finally, Charlie broke the silence. "It's morning," he said. "Is it obvious now what we're supposed to do?"

I had been thinking about it, and the Druid was right. I didn't want him to be right, but we had no other choice. "We go to Fyren's hideout," I said.

"Who are you to make our decisions for us?"

Charlie asked. He wasn't in good humour.

"I'm not making the decision. It's been made for us. We don't know the way to the village, but we have a clear path back to Fyren's. There's nothing else we can do."

"He's right," Pendragon said. "We could wander this forest for days and never find our way out."

"Won't they come looking for us?"

"They will, but fear of the dragon will keep them from coming this far. And if they do, Fyren will be ready for them."

Charlie stood and kicked at the dirt. "So, it is obvious after all, just like that old man said."

"Perhaps he is to be trusted," Pendragon said.

"Then we all agree?" I asked.

Charlie shrugged. "I'm hungry," he said. "Maybe there'll be food there."

We knew what to do, but we weren't in a hurry to leave. We stayed at the fire until it died down, then we covered it with dirt and followed Pendragon into the forest.

It was slow going. Pendragon kept insisting that we move more quietly, even though we were being as careful as we could. Any chance we had of succeeding depended on us getting back to Fyren's hideout without being spotted by the lookouts. Only Pendragon had the ability to do that, but he couldn't leave us behind, so the three of us crept forward at an agonizingly slow pace, stopping, starting, looking, listening. I could tell Charlie was getting annoyed, and Pendragon was skittish as a deer, and we were all afraid. If keeping silent hadn't been so important, we'd have probably ended up shouting at each other.

An hour went by, then two, and then light rain

began to fall. Incredibly, this lifted Pendragon's spirits.

"This will cover our approach," he said. "The rain will be louder than the noise you make."

"Oh, so it's our fault?" Charlie asked.

"He's right," I said, before it could escalate. "He knows how to do this, we don't"

"Well, I'm still not happy about the rain."

Pendragon ignored him. "Hopefully, it will last, and get heavier."

It didn't, but the constant drizzle soon soaked us to the skin. I hugged myself for warmth, but it didn't stop me shivering.

When we finally arrived at the rise overlooking the hideout, Pendragon manoeuvred us to a spot under a tree, which kept us hidden and sheltered us from the rain, at least a little bit. The open area in front of the hill looked empty and untouched, revealing no hint of the activity that had taken place the previous day. Leaves covered the ground, and the fire pit had been hidden under a spiny bush. The hideout itself was invisible. With its door and windows covered, it appeared to be a massive, impenetrable jumble of weeds and briers lining the base of the rocky bluff. Above the hideout, the hill was mostly bare, covered only in patches of grass or hardy weeds. It rose about fifty feet and served as an unmanned fortress, making approach from the rear impossible.

"Stay here and keep watch," Pendragon said. "Make no noise. Do not move."

"You're leaving us?" Charlie asked.

"There are lookouts. We need to know where they are. I will not be long."

He left before we could object, moving silently through the wood.

"I don't think he likes us," Charlie said.

"I think he thinks we're going to get him killed. You have to admit, we're a liability. He's a lot better at this than we are."

Charlie wiped the rain from his face. "Maybe we should have joined the Boy Scouts, like Dad wanted. They do stuff like this."

"Yeah, they might have taught us to make a fire by rubbing two sticks together."

The mention of fire only made us colder, so we settle down to watch. Nothing happened, and there was nothing we could do except get colder and wait for Pendragon.

I started to feel bad for him. He hadn't asked for this, and we weren't being much help. I tried to think of a way we could be of use. We might not be able to start a fire or sneak silently through the woods, but we had to have some worthwhile abilities. We didn't have any modern technology with us, but we did have modern knowledge; that had to count for something. Currently, however, our job was to watch, which was the least we could do.

I calculated that the thieves numbered around a dozen. That was the number we had seen the previous day, although there might have been others inside. There was no sign of them now, however. As far as anyone could tell, there was no one around. The hideout might even be empty. Perhaps they'd moved on. I continued to look for any signs that the hideout might be inhabited but found none.

When Pendragon finally returned, he confirmed that the thieves were definitely there.

"Three lookouts," he said. "All watching in the direction of the village."

"What about behind?"

Pendragon shook his head. "No one can come from that way. We'll have to go in through the front."

"How?" Charlie asked.

"None of the lookouts were checking behind them. If we can move around the clearing and get between the lookouts and Fyren's den, we should be able to reach it without being seen."

"Unless the ones inside have holes to look through," I said.

Pendragon nodded. "It is possible."

"What difference does it make?" Charlie asked. "We get there seen, or unseen, and then what do we do? Knock on the door as ask if we can have our cloak back? And, oh, I hear you have something called the Talisman, can you give that to us, too?"

No one answered. We just stared at the thicket, trying to come up with a plan that didn't have 'suicide' written all over it.

For a long time, no one spoke, then Pendragon said, "We need to do something soon. The lookouts will not stay at their posts all day. If they are replaced, the new ones will be more alert. We want to move when the lookouts are tired and cold."

I rubbed my arms for warmth and tried to stop shivering. "Right now, I think I'm ready to just walk up and ask if we could come inside to get warm."

"Yeah," Charlie said. "I bet they've got a fire going in there."

Then I remembered what the Druid had told us. "That's the flaw," I said. "They're sure to have a fire in there."

"So?" Charlie asked.

"So, where's the smoke going?"

Pendragon nodded and looked toward the hideout. "He's right."

"A chimney," I said. "There'll be a chimney somewhere. We need to find it."

Chapter 15

We backtracked, then moved in a wide circle to get to the other side of the hill without alerting the lookouts. From behind, there was a steep slope, but no sharp incline to indicate where the forest floor ended and the hill began. It was thick with trees and shrubs but also dotted with rocky outcrops. We climbed cautiously, watching for lookouts. There may have been no reason for them to be looking our way, but it didn't mean they weren't, so our climb took a lot longer than it should have. We were nearly to the top when I noticed mist rising from a cluster of boulders.

I tapped Pendragon's shoulder and pointed. "What's that?"

"Smoke," Pendragon said. "It could be someone sheltering among the rocks, or it might be what we're looking for."

Once more, Pendragon left us hidden while he went to look. He returned shortly, a smile on his face.

"It's an opening," he said.

The opening was small. Too small for a full-grown man to fit through, which gave us an advantage. Pendragon went first. He seemed to think he was in charge of the expedition, and I wasn't going to argue. He'd gotten us this far.

He had some difficulty squeezing through, but soon he disappeared. Then his voice echoed out of the tunnel. "It widens down here. See if you can fit through.

I went in, feet first, choking as the smoke swirled around me. I wriggled my way into the hole, scraping my back as my tee shirt rode up to my shoulders. Then I popped through. Pendragon was right, the passage opened up. A little.

"C'mon, Charlie."

Pendragon moved down the passage and I followed, making room for Charlie, who had more difficulty getting through than I did. He groaned and twisted and said a few words Mom wouldn't have been happy about but eventually he got through.

"At least it's warmer here," he said, following us down.

The passage wasn't man-made, so it didn't go straight up and down. It was more of a twisted slant, a natural passageway that had to end up, we hoped, somewhere in Fyren's lair.

Rain had trickled in, so the rocks were moist and slick, which made progress difficult. Also, we had to keep from coughing from the smoke. We picked our way cautiously along the slippery rock until the light from the opening disappeared. I waved my hand in front of my face. It was just like in the forest the previous night. Below me, Pendragon edged forward. And we followed.

In the darkness came the clack of falling rocks, a yelp, and a thud.

"Pendragon, are you all right?"

"Yes. The passage opens to a cavern. There is a drop. Be cautious."

I felt my way forward, then slipped through an opening. Thanks to Pendragon's warning, I managed to land on my feet. Moments later, Charlie landed next to me.

"Where are we?" he asked.

I reached around in the darkness, then raised my hands as far as I could, feeling nothing but the wafting of the smoky air being sucked up the chimney. "I think the better question is, 'how do we get out of here?'"

"There's a passage," Pendragon said. "Come this way."

I felt my way forward in the inky blackness until I found a wall, then followed it toward Pendragon's voice. When I got to him, the wall ended. "There's an opening," I said.

"Yes, and another over here," Charlie said.

"How do we know which one to take?" I asked.

"There is fresh air coming through this one," Pendragon said. "Can you smell it? This leads to the outside."

I nodded. So, they had a back door. It made sense. It also made sense that it was guarded. But we'd have to worry about that later.

In the darkness, Charlie shuffled closer. "If there are multiple tunnels here, any one of them might lead to more tunnels. Which one goes to the hideout?"

"That's easy," I said. "Follow the smoke."

We made better time in the passageway than the chimney. It was larger and nearly level so all we had to do was feel along the wall. Soon, we saw a faint glow ahead, and heard muffled voices. As we crept forward, toward the light, the voices grew louder and the smoke grew thicker, mingling with the scent of cooked meat. When the end of the passage came in sight, we saw it was partly covered by a curtain. It hung about a third of the way down, letting smoke through the opening, and making a sort of door over the rest.

We laid down and cautiously lifted the bottom of the curtain about an inch and peered through.

What we saw looked like a dishevelled Aladdin's cave. It was dim, lit by a fire and several torches, but they provided enough light for us to see, and what we saw amazed us. All around, hanging on the walls, suspended from ropes or lying in heaps on the floor were fine garments, animal skins, silver cups, plates, candlesticks, and leather bags that looked like they contained money. Lying up against the wall were piles of straw and tattered blankets. The fire was near the opening, far from the outer wall, spitting and popping, the low flames heating a big slab of meat suspended from a sturdy metal frame. At the end of the room, furthest from the smoking fire, a group of men sat at a rickety table, drinking from gold and silver chalices. They were laughing and talking so loudly that we didn't worry about being heard or seen.

I raised the blanket a bit more to get a better view. "This place is massive."

Saplings, tied together with ropes, formed the walls of the room, and bent into the hillside to form the roof. Branches, straw, and leaves were woven into the frame to give the illusion of a giant, impenetrable thicket. The reason no one came close enough to uncover the illusion was hanging from a wooden frame next to the table where the men sat—the dragon. Unmanned and up close, it was a wonder it fooled anybody. The limp body was nothing but stiff blankets with strips of green material sewn onto it. The head was leather, crudely shaped to form horns, eyes, and a conical snout. The eye holes were empty.

"What should we do now?" Charlie asked.

"I don't know," I said. "I don't see our cloak."

"I don't see Fyren, either," Pendragon said.

The men at the table continued their boisterous conversation and didn't look our way. But it seemed they were purposely not looking our way, and their conversation sounded stilted, like they were pretending to talk.

"There's only six," Charlie said. "Where are the others?"

Pendragon jumped up. "Run."

Chapter 16

The blanket whipped aside, flooding the passageway with light. We turned to run but found ourselves facing Fyren, who was wearing our cloak. Behind him, two other men blocked the passageway. Before I could think to run in the opposite direction, rough hands grabbed my neck, arms, and legs. I wriggled and shouted but couldn't break free. They carried me, along with Pendragon and Charlie, into the room and threw us face down on the hard-packed earth. More men came in from the tunnel, others through the door to the outside. Then a heavy hand pressed my face into the dirt.

Gradually, the commotion stopped and the only sound I heard was my own breathing.

"Well, what have we here?"

The hand let go and I raised my head. Fyren, no longer looking like an old man, stood in front of us. His clothes were coarse but neat and our cloak floated around him, giving him a regal aura.

"We should kill them now," one of the thieves said. "They know our secret."

Fyren shook his head. "No. I believe they will prove useful to us. Secure them."

One of Fyren's men pulled my arms behind my back and lashed them with twine. Then we were all dragged closer to the fire and arranged in a row, with our feet bound as well as our hands. Fyren came and stood between us and the fire.

"You are the boys from whom I received this cloak."

"You stole it from us," Charlie said.

Fyren bent down, his face close to Charlie's. "You are very brave to come this far."

"It's our cloak. We need it back."

Fyren stood. "I expect you do. But that's not going to happen." He stepped in front of me, inspecting my clothes as if he was a drill sergeant and I was on parade. "Your attire, it is unusual. And, of course, you once owned this cloak. This makes me think you have come for the Talisman."

The room went silent. I looked up at Fyren. "What's a Talisman?"

Fyren unhooked a leather pouch from his belt. "Don't play games. Mordred sent you. That's the only way you could have acquired this cloak."

"Grandfather gave it—"

Fyren kicked my legs. Hard. "Enough." He untied the laces holding the bag closed and pulled out a black stone. If that was the Talisman, it wasn't as impressive as I had imagined. It was a disk, about the size of a hockey puck, but thinner. And it was the deepest black I had ever seen. So dark it appeared to suck the light from around it. Fyren held it up, gazing into it.

"Mordred commissioned me to steal this for him," he said, "but before I could hand it over, the stone spoke to me." He crouched and gazed at Pendragon, Charlie and then me, staring at us with dark, glistening eyes. "I am its Guardian now," he whispered. "And its power will make me king of thieves and bring me great wealth."

Fyren looked up at the men standing behind us. "Untie them. Just their hands. And watch them closely."

The rope loosened and I brought my hands forward, massaging my wrists.

"Now," Fyren said, "we will see what you are truly about." Without warning, he shoved the stone into my hands. "Look into it."

"What?"

"Look into it. See if it speaks to you. See what it tells you."

I looked down at the stone. It was smooth as a mirror, but I didn't see a reflection. It was more like peering into a hole, a hole that went on and on and on. I realized it was drawing me in. I felt light-headed, mesmerized, and my fingers, where they touched the Talisman, began to tingle. And then I saw an image. Faint, but growing stronger, more defined. My eyes widened, trying to take it in, to interpret its meaning.

Fyren snatched the stone from my hand. "What did you see?"

I blinked and shook my head, slowly coming back to myself. "Water," I whispered, still not understanding what I had seen, or why.

"Ha," Fyren shouted, slapping his thigh. "The power of the universe at your fingertips and all you want is a drink. The Talisman favours you, but you have no imagination." He went to a barrel standing next to the fire, which was now mostly glowing coals. "Here is what the Talisman promised you." He took a ladle hanging from the side of the barrel, dipped it in and carried it, dripping beads of water, back to me. "Was this what you were shown?" He held the ladle to my lips. I was thirsty and strained forward, trying to reach it.

Fyren laughed. He pulled the ladle away and poured the water on the coals. It hissed and spit and threw billows of steam into the air.

My arms were wrenched behind me again, and my hands bound.

Fyren moved to Charlie and handed him the stone. Charlie gazed into it as I had done, staring into the depths of the black hole, until he, too, saw something. I knew he must have had the same experience I'd had because his eyes opened wide in surprise. The moment they did, Fyren grabbed the Talisman.

"Fire," Charlie said, without being asked. "I saw fire."

Fyren grinned and nodded. "Then the Talisman did show you your future. For there is definitely fire in it." He chuckled and moved on to Pendragon, who had been watching intently.

Pendragon held the stone for a few moments, staring into it. He kept his eyes narrowed and his brow furrowed, as if in deep concentration. Then he handed the Talisman back to Fyren and shook his head. "I saw nothing."

Fyren stood. "No doubt," he said, putting the Talisman back into the pouch. "You are not one of the cloak bearers. But they have seen true." He looked at Charlie. "Fire it is. You will roast, one by one, so the last will get to hear the others scream, and then we will set your charred bodies where the villagers can find them. That will keep them flapping their gobs about the dragon for many months to come, and stop them from becoming too curious."

The men who had stood silently behind us while Fyren talked now began to move about, laughing and talking to one another. They grabbed us and pushed us close to the fire while others piled more sticks and logs on it. Soon flames were leaping, and it became uncomfortably hot. Two of the thieves lifted the meat from the fire, and pulled it from the bar that had been holding it

"Don't worry," one of the thieves said, "before your roasting, we'll drive this through you." He grinned and held up the iron bar, which was sharpened at one end. When he was certain we'd seen it, he stood it up against the wall near the fire pit, then he pointed at the metal frame the meat had been cooking on. "You might still be alive when we hang you up there, but you won't be for long."

"Decide amongst yourselves who wants to go first," said another. "It will be harder to go last. Hearing your companions scream would be most horrible. Best to go quick, eh?"

The thieves left us in front of the fire and congregated around the table, with Fyren sitting at the head. They threw the meat on a big, silver platter and tore at it with hands and knives. Jugs of beer appeared, and one of the thieves returned to fetch loaves of bread from a shelf in the wall behind the fire.

"You'll have plenty of time to decide who goes first," he said, winking at us. "We need a nice bed of coals to cook you evenly. That's going to take a while. But try not to think about it too much."

He laughed and joined his companions at the table and soon the room was filled with laughter and shouts and the scent of roasted meat.

No one spoke for a while. We just sat, staring into the fire.

"I don't think this is what Granddad had in mind,"

I said, wondering what would happen. Would we wake up back in Wynantskill or, if this was really real, would we end up really dead?

"I lied to him," Pendragon said, staring into the fire.

"What? Did you see something?"

Pendragon nodded, as if he was half asleep and still staring into the Talisman. "Yes," he said, "I saw a line of descendants, reaching far into the future." He turned to look at me. "And it's true, I know it is."

"So that means?" Charlie asked.

"That we're not going to die here. But I couldn't let Fyren know, or he'd have killed us on the spot."

"Then what it showed you was useful," Charlie said. "So maybe what it showed me …" He looked into the fire that was now getting painfully hot. "I have an idea."

Our legs were bound in front of us and our hands behind, so it was difficult to move, but Charlie inched himself forward, even closer to the fire.

"What are you doing?" Pendragon asked.

Charlie moved closer. "Shh!" he said. "Keep an eye out. Make sure no one is looking."

Using his feet, Charlie teased a stick out of the fire, dragging it with the heel of his sneaker until the glowing end was lying on the dirt. Then he held his feet over the stick, touching the twine around his ankles to the coals.

Fortunately, the twine didn't catch fire. The glowing coal burned into the fibres, blackening them and sending up smoke. Soon, one of the strands broke. Charlie worked his feet free, then scuttled back from the flames.

"Do you want us to try that?" I asked.

"No," he said, "just keep me covered."

With his feet free, Charlie could move a little easier. He inched forward to the fire and grabbed another stick with his feet. Then he pulled it well back and moved forward again until the stick was behind him.

"This is the part I'm not too sure about," he said. "Help me get my hands over it, so I can burn the ropes."

He pulled his hands apart as far as he could and awkwardly moved them around, trying to find the stick.

"A bit to your left," I said. "Down, just a little."

"Ow!"

"I said, a little."

Charlie's skin was so close to the stick I was afraid he'd sear himself, but the twine took most of the heat. Charlie twisted and pulled and soon it frayed and broke.

We all sat still, with Charlie maintaining his position, until we were sure no one was watching. Then Charlie slid next to me and undid my hands. He then moved to Pendragon and undid his. Still, we didn't move. When we were sure no one was watching, Pendragon leaned forward and untied his feet. Then I did the same.

"Now what do we do?" I asked, staring straight ahead and keeping my voice low.

"What the Talisman told us to do," Charlie said. "You saw water, right?"

I thought about what I had seen. It was just water, gushing, cascading, but from where? And to where? I hadn't had time to see it properly. And there wasn't any water around, anyway. Then I remembered the barrel standing near the fire. "I've got it," I said.

Charlie nodded. "Okay, move fast, fire first, then

water. Ready?"

"No," Pendragon said, but Charlie was already moving. He grabbed the sticks near the base of the fire, pulled them out and flung them around the room. One after another he pulled and threw, into the blankets, the piles of clothing and the heaps of straw. The thieves scrambled toward us. Charlie pulled the last few sticks from the fire and threw them into the latticework of the walls and ceiling. Pendragon grabbed the iron bar they were going to skewer us with and flung it lengthwise at the approaching men. It hit the first three in the chest, who fell onto the ones behind. Others jumped over them and rushed at us. Then I tipped the water barrel onto the fire.

It was heavy and didn't budge at first. I had to lean into it, straining with all my strength, which was helped by my being so scared. The barrel tilted, then momentum took hold and it fell on its side, gushing water, as if a miniature dam had burst. The wave washed over the heap of coals.

Immediately, the room filled with hissing steam. Hidden by the fog, we jumped aside as the men lunged forward, tripping over the barrel. Some fell into the fire, others slipped on the wet ground. Screams of pain and frustration rose from the mist.

"Quick," I said. "Find Fyren."

The room began to fill with smoke as the scattered fires caught hold. Some of the thieves grabbed at the burning piles of clothing, trying to salvage what they could. Others filled their arms with silverware as fire leapt up the walls and scuttled across the ceiling.

"To the tunnel," someone yelled. "Take what you can, save yourselves."

Fyren's voice came out of the fog. "No, you

cowards," he shouted. "The boys. Capture the boys."

"That's Fyren," Charlie said. "Come on."

We rushed into the smoke and mist, toward the voice, and ran full speed into Fyren. We all tumbled to the ground, with Fyren beneath us. He struggled to get up, but Charlie pushed him down by the shoulders and knelt on his chest. Pendragon grabbed the knife from Fyren's belt and held it to his throat. "Get the cloak, and his bag," he shouted.

"Help me," Fyren shouted.

I yanked the leather pouch containing the Talisman from Fyren's belt, Charlie unclasped the cloak. "I can't get it off him," he said, "he's lying on it."

I pushed Charlie aside. "I've got an idea." I jumped up and landed, on my knees, on Fyren's chest. His eyes popped open, he whooshed a gust of breath and started gasping.

"It's what Pete did to me," I said. "It hurts like hell and you can't get your breath. Hurry, we've only got about fifteen seconds."

We rolled him roughly onto his face and I yanked the cloak off him.

"Quick, the window."

Pendragon rammed his shoulder into the wall, dislodging the window covering.

"Go, go," I shouted.

Pendragon dove headfirst through the opening. Charlie followed, holding the leather bag. Then I ran, clumsily bundling the cloak, and tried to jump, but a hand grabbed me from behind.

I threw the cloak at the window where it hung, half in, half out.

"Help," I shouted.

"Get over here, you fools," Fyren screamed.

"They're getting away."

I struggled forward, grabbing for the cloak as Charlie pulled it from the outside. I held on as Fyren held me, both of us inching forward. Then a hand grabbed mine and pulled. My arms and head went out the window, but Fyren still gripped my legs. Fresh air swirled around me, sucked in by the hungry flames. Over the roaring of the fire, I heard the sounds of shouting and pounding feet.

"Kick him," Pendragon shouted.

I flailed out as hard as I could and connected with something. A cry of pain and anger came from behind and Fyren's grip loosened. Pendragon and Charlie grabbed my arms and pulled.

The three of us, the cloak and the Talisman tumbled to the ground. Several sets of hands reached through the window, but they were blocking their own way. The hideout now looked like a huge thicket that was on fire. Smoke seeped through the branches and leaves, then flames shot up, first in one place, then another, and another. Inside, the men shouted. Fyren loudest of all.

We jumped up and ran.

Chapter 17

We raced into the forest, heading for the rise where we had kept watch.

"Look for the trail markers," Pendragon shouted, rushing ahead of us.

Charlie and I ran faster, struggling to keep up.

"That won't lead us to the village," I said, my lungs already burning.

"It will lead us away from here."

I was the furthest behind, struggling to hold the cloak. As I crested the rise, I chanced a look over my shoulder. The hideout was fully ablaze, but the front door was open and several men, with Fyren in the lead, were running after us.

"No time," I shouted. "Just run."

For a moment, as we careened down the far side, we were out of sight of our pursuers. Pendragon turned away from the trail. "This way."

We ran into the forest, jumping logs, ducking under branches, dodging around bushes, trying to get as far into whatever cover the woods could provide before Fyren and his men saw us. We blundered forward as fast as we could, not caring about the noise. Behind us, angry shouts covered our escape. Then the shouting stopped. Pendragon brought us to a halt.

"They're listening," he said. "Move quietly."

I could tell from his expression that he didn't hold

out much hope. We followed behind him, trying to move like he did, with hardly a sound, but it was hopeless. I kept stumbling, trying to keep from tripping over the cloak. Then Charlie stepped on a large twig. In the quiet forest, the snap sounded like rifle fire.

"Over there," came a shout.

"Quickly," Pendragon said.

We ran in a different direction, hoping to throw them off. The shouting behind us grew closer.

"This way," Pendragon said.

He led us toward a small hill, and we followed as fast as we could.

"If we can get over the top without them seeing us, we might be able to hide from them."

As plans go, it wasn't a good one, but it was all we had. We scrambled up the side of the hill, trying to make as little noise as possible, hoping to get to the other side before someone saw us.

Then came another shout. "Over here."

"They've seen us," Pendragon said. But he didn't slow down. We got to the top and ran down the other side. And saw horses.

There, in front of us, wearing a breastplate and sitting on his horse, his standard bearer beside him, was Fergus. Spread out on the valley floor, all mounted and dressed for battle, were half a dozen men.

Fergus walked his horse forward.

"Help us," I said.

Fergus looked at Charlie, holding the leather bag, and me holding the cloak. Then he smiled. "You beg my protection?"

"We need your help," Charlie said. "There are men coming this way. Thieves. They want to kill us."

"So," Fergus said, more slowly. "Will you swear

fealty?"

Pendragon, who had been in front of us, took a step back to stand between me and Charlie. "It's a trick," he said quietly. "He'll want the cloak."

"We just need help, that's all," I said. "We're not swearing fealty or anything."

Fergus nodded. "Very well."

He turned his horse and signalled to his men. All of them turned around and began riding away. Behind us, the shouting drew nearer.

"You can't just leave us," I shouted.

Fergus looked over his shoulder. "You are no concern of mine. If you swear fealty, I will be obligated to protect you. Otherwise ..." He shrugged and kept riding. The shouts were closer now, coming up the far side of the hill.

"All right," I said. "We swear fealty."

"No," Pendragon said.

"We have to. Fyren will kill us. Then Fergus will kill him, and he'll still have our cloak only we'll be dead."

"If this is a dream, I'd really like to wake up now," Charlie said.

"So, you swear?" Fergus asked. "All of you?"

Fyren and his men gained the summit and rushed down toward us.

"Yes," I said. "Whatever, but just help us, please."

Fergus raised a hand and called to his men. The sound of the men rushing down the slope toward us became drowned by the pounding of hooves.

"Take Fyren alive," Fergus shouted as his knights thundered up the slope. They met the thieves halfway, then galloped on as they scattered, screaming.

Fergus looked down at us. "Amazing. You managed to escape."

"You knew we were in there?" I asked. "And you didn't try to save us?"

"I was waiting for an opportune moment," Fergus said.

"You were—" Charlie began, but a sharp elbow to the ribs from Pendragon stopped him.

"Your friend is wise," Fergus said. "You must learn to speak respectfully to a knight, especially if he is your master."

"Our master," Charlie sputtered.

"Yes," Pendragon said. "You swore fealty. Now we belong to him."

Fergus nodded, smiling. "And all you possess. Give the cloak and the bag to me."

"But the cloak is ours," I said. "And the bag, we need to give that—"

"To me," Fergus said. "They are mine by right, as are you. You are now my pages, and all you have is mine. Now turn them over and stand behind." Fergus turned to his standard bearer. "Relieve them of my possessions."

Charlie gripped the bag and held it to his chest. "Pages? What's he talking about?"

"Servants," Pendragon said.

"Slaves," I added.

The standard bearer dismounted and drove the standard pole into the ground. Then he took the cloak from me and Fyren's leather bag from Charlie and handed them up to Fergus.

"The cloak at last has a worthy owner," Fergus said, swinging the cloak over his shoulders and fastening it around his neck. He opened the bag and pulled out the Talisman, turning it slowly in his fingers, staring into it.

"Get behind," the standard bearer shouted, kicking

out at us. "Eyes off the master, stand and wait."

So, we stood behind Fergus, and waited.

"I always thought I should like to be a page," Pendragon whispered. "But I think this is going to be unpleasant."

Soon the horsemen returned, some with saddle bags bulging with the silver and gold the thieves had been trying to carry away, and one leading a captive—Fyren—tied by the wrists and tethered to a horse.

The horsemen, leading Fyren, came to Fergus. "Some of the thieves have disappeared into the wood," he said. "Their den is destroyed, with all that was in it. What we have recovered we got from the fleeing thieves."

I didn't want to know what had happened to the thieves they did catch. The fact that they hadn't taken them prisoner said enough.

Fergus looked down at Fyren. "What say you now? Do you still revel in your deceit?"

"My pact was with Mordred," Fyren said. "It is for Mordred to come for the Talisman, not you."

"Your cheek knows no bounds. Mordred is, himself, searching the land for you, because you fled with the Talisman. Had he found you, he would have had you drawn and quartered."

Fyren shrank back a little. "I trust you will be more merciful," he said.

Fergus smiled. "I will be, but merely because I am in haste." He looked at the man guarding Fyren. "Hang him."

Fyren's shoulders drooped. The knight on the horse dismounted and led him a short way into the woods. Other knights came, some on foot, others on horses. One threw a rope over a low limb. Fyren struggled as they put a noose around his neck.

I didn't want to see it, but I couldn't look away. "Are they really going to hang him?" I asked.

Pendragon nodded. "It is the penalty. He knew this would happen one day."

"No," I said. "I think he believed the Talisman when it told him he would be the king of thieves. I think this is coming as quite a surprise."

"He's not making a sound," Charlie said. "I'd be begging for my life."

"He is grateful for not being drawn and quartered," Pendragon said. "Hanging is a mercy compared to that."

Fergus, and all the men with him, turned to look as three knights hauled on the rope and Fyren's feet left the ground. He thrashed and grunted. A stain spread over the front of his tunic. I turned away and saw Charlie had done the same. Pendragon, however, continued to watch.

After an agonizingly long time, the grunting became quieter. Then it stopped. I turned to look. Fyren still hung from the branch, swaying lazily, his arms limp at his side, his head bowed, his tongue, swollen and purple, protruding from his open mouth. Next to me, Charlie groaned.

"Do you still think this is a dream?" I asked.

Chapter 18

The best thing about being taken captive by Fergus was that we finally got some warmer clothes. The rest, not so good.

Once they were sure Fyren was dead, Fergus sent two of his men back to the hideout to see if they could find more of Fyren's men. And, of course, any treasure that remained. He also sent one of his squires back to the village to tell them how he, Fergus, had bravely slain the dragon. Then the rest of the company trotted off, with the three of us accompanying them.

They didn't tie us up, but Fergus made sure there were two men behind us on horseback, urging us forward. They told us that if we ran, they would ride us down, which didn't sound fun. They needn't have worried. We weren't going anywhere, not as long as Fergus had our cloak, and the Talisman.

We headed south. I only knew this because I heard Fergus shout a command. It wasn't raining any more, but it was still cloudy and there was no sun and, after the heat from the fire and the terror of the escape, I was beginning to shiver again. That's why when, a short time later, we arrived at a clearing in the wood— where other pages and squires waited with the pack horses—I was glad to get some new clothes.

We stood at the edge of the activity, trying to keep out of the way when one of the pages threw a bundle at us. It hit me in the chest and almost knocked me over. I wasn't sure what was going on until I picked it up and saw it was a smock, like Pendragon was wearing, and a pair of pants made from the same rough material. Then the boy threw another bundle at Charlie. But he caught it.

"Sir Fergus will not have you wearing those garments," the boy said. "Put these on. And what sort of boots have you?"

"Nike," Charlie said.

"What ever they are, take them off."

Charlie shook his head. "No way. They're practically new. And I like them."

The boy scowled at us through strands of greasy hair that hung to his shoulders, the style that most in the group seemed to favour. He was older than us, but younger than the squires. He was also bigger, with thick arms, calloused hands, and a round belly. He could have forced us, one at a time, but we were three to his one and I could tell he was calculating the odds of being able to take us all on at once.

"I'd rather keep them," I said, hoping to ease the tension. "I don't think Fergus would mind. We could ask him."

"Sir Fergus!" the boy shouted. "I am head page boy. You do not talk to Sir Fergus. You talk to me."

"Then go ask him," Charlie said. He'd already put the smock on over his tee shirt and now he pulled the loose pants over his shorts. "If he wants us to give up our sneakers then we will, okay with you, buddy?"

"My name is Eadwig," the boy sputtered.

"Earwig?" I asked, not meaning to be impolite; that's what I thought he'd said.

The boy's face went red. "Eadwig," he said. Then

he pushed me. It seemed like a gentle movement for him, but it left me sprawling on the ground. "Remember it well."

He left us then. I got up and put on my new clothes. I say new—they were dirty and smelly and didn't fit comfortably, but at least they were warm.

"He could make trouble for us," Pendragon said.

"He's not going to Fergus," Charlie said. "I may not know much about your customs, but I know a child isn't going to go tattling on us to a knight.

"He doesn't need to go to Sir Fergus to be trouble," Pendragon said.

We didn't have time to think about it. The knights and squires mounted up and the whole group, nearly thirty in all, moved on, with the pages walking behind the pack horses. Eadwig kept his distance, but I noticed him glancing my way from time to time.

Walking through the forest with all those people and horses and sacks of supplies was slow. It was also boring, and tiring. Eventually, we came to a path just wide enough for a man or a horse. After that, even though we had to walk in single file, it got a little faster. But it was still boring and tiresome.

Gradually, the forest thinned and turned into fields and bushy meadows. There, the going was easier. The knights and squires rode side by side and we were able to bunch up with the rest of the pages. As we walked, they passed water skins around occasionally, which helped, but I was still hungry and ready to drop by the time we reached the road.

It looked like the one that Pendragon had led us to—raised, straight and made of stones—but this one was in better condition, and it was wider. The company stopped in a field at the edge of the road. The knights and squires dismounted. The pages clustered around the pack horses, untying bags and opening bundles.

Pendragon sat. "I think they're going to make camp."

Charlie and I flopped down beside him. "I hope so," I said, leaning back on the grass and closing my eyes. "I can't walk another step."

I enjoyed my rest for approximately ten seconds. Then someone kicked me in the side.

"Get up!"

It was Eadwig.

"Why?"

"Work to do? Do you think you're a Lord?"

I sat up, rubbing my side. "We're prisoners. Prisoners don't work."

Eadwig shook his head. "You are page boys. Sir Fergus' page boys. So, get up."

Being the new boys, they gave us the easy jobs, like digging the latrines and hauling firewood, while the others erected tents and tended the fires. I noticed the hard work was done by the pages. The squires did the easier work, like cooking and serving drinks to the knights, who did nothing but sit around their fire talking and laughing.

Soon, the knights Fergus had sent back to Fyren's hideout returned carrying a few more sacks filled with stolen items. Then the squire arrived, and assured Fergus that the villagers were grateful, and forever in his debt. If Aisley and Garberend had asked him about their missing son, he didn't say.

There wasn't any water to wash in, so by the time we were ordered to serve the knights dinner, we had to bring it to them muddy and stinking. I felt embarrassed at first, but no one took any notice of us. We weren't important enough to be visible and everyone smelled of something, so we moved in and around the knights and none of them seemed to mind. I minded. All I wanted was a hot shower and a warm bed, but as soon as we were done serving the knights, we had to start cleaning up, and that lasted until it began to get dark. Then, finally, we were allowed a bit of bread and some hard cheese.

And our day didn't end there. We had to keep the knights supplied with wine and beer as the day darkened and their talking grew more raucous. Finally, hours later, the fires died down, the knights retired to their tents, and we were allowed to sleep.

None of us had spoken for hours. We'd simply gone from task to task like zombies, moving, always moving, because if we stopped, we'd fall down and never get up. Pendragon didn't look as bad as Charlie and I did, but he was just as glad for the rest. We found an open bit of grass near one of the flickering fires, slumped down and fell immediately into a deep sleep.

Chapter 19

A sharp pain in my side jarred me awake. I grunted and opened my eyes just in time to see Eadwig getting ready to kick me again.

"Hey, stop—"

"There's work to do," he said, landing another blow with his boot. "You are not sleeping the day away."

I tried to sit up. Every single inch of my body hurt. My feet were sore, my legs ached, my arms felt like they were on fire, my hands were blistered, it hurt to breathe, and over it all was the deep burning in my side where Eadwig had kicked me.

"What are we supposed to do?" My voice rasped. Until then, I didn't know even speaking could hurt.

"Gather wood for the fires," he said. "Then tend the horses."

Eadwig walked away. The camp was coming alive, with a few fires already going and the boys running back and forth, some packing up, others cooking over sputtering flames. Our fire was nothing but cold ash. I was covered in dew and, now that I was awake, I began to shiver. At least the dew meant the day wasn't cloudy. The sky was blue and brightening, and the sun was getting ready to rise over the distant trees.

Charlie rolled onto his back and yawned. "What's going on?"

"We need to get up. My new best friend Earwig says

we have work to do."

"Every molecule in my body hurts," Charlie said. "I'm tired, and wet, and cold. Remind me to thank Granddad if we ever get back home."

"Some work will get you warm," Pendragon said, rising and stretching and—I noticed with mild irritation—not wincing at all, "and a fire will dry you."

It was agony getting to my feet, and walking only made it worse, but I thought it would be best to keep any complaints to myself. Apparently, Charlie felt the same. He limped along beside me but didn't say a word.

There were stands of trees nearby and we found some wood there. Pendragon started our fire while we distributed the little we had to the other page boys, most of whom ignored us or merely grunted. Then we went to tend the horses. I hoped that Pendragon would know what to do because I had no idea.

The horses were near the edge of the camp, tied to trees and stakes in the ground. The ropes were long enough for them to graze, so they didn't look hungry. There was one horse for each of the seven knights, one for each of the seven squires, and an additional five to carry the supplies and baggage, so nineteen in all, a mixture of grey and brown, and every one of them—Pendragon informed us—were mares, except one.

Tied to a tree just beyond the group of mares was the horse Fergus rode, a stallion. He was bigger than the others, dark brown, almost black, with a diamond of white between his eyes, and he didn't look as friendly. He watched us as we approached the group of mares, snorting and stamping the ground with his hoof.

"We'd best handle the mares first," Pendragon said, casting a concerned glance at the stallion.

"What are we supposed to be doing?" Charlie asked.

Pendragon looked at him, puzzled. "They need water."

He seemed surprised we didn't know this, as surprised as I was that he did, because no one had told us that.

We knew which direction the water was in because we'd seen some of the other page boys going out with empty water skins and returning with full ones. The problem was getting the water to the horses, or the horses to the water.

"We'll lead them two at a time," Pendragon said. He apparently had appointed himself foreman, but I wasn't about to argue. I'd seen horses before, but I'd never been this close to one, and I'd never thought I'd be leading them around by a rope.

"What if they try to get away from us?" Charlie asked.

It was a good question, but the one I wanted answered was, what do we do if they try to kill us?

Pendragon didn't answer. He just untied the horses and handed us each two ropes. I gripped them tight, feeling so nervous I forgot how cold and sore I was. The horses didn't try to run away, though. They just stood behind me, so close I could feel their breath on the back of my neck, closer even than when we had visited that farm with Mom and Dad. I'd been eight, and the farmer had led the horse across the corral to all the kids who had gathered at the fence. The horse had poked his snout through the fence and Charlie, along with a dozen other kids, had stroked his nose while I had backed away, terrified that the huge, smelly beast would trample me. At that time, scared as I was, I at least had a fence to protect me. Now, I was holding two of them, by myself, with no idea what I was supposed to do with them.

Then Pendragon said, "Follow me." So, I did.

To my amazement the horses ambled along with me. It was slow and easy, and soothing to be in the fresh air, feeling the warming sun and not having anyone kicking me.

The water—a wide stream—was a short walk from the camp. We let the horses drink for a while, then led them back. Pendragon showed us how to secure them, then we untied another group of six and led them away. By the time we brought the final group, I was no longer as nervous. The horses seemed docile, and willing to be led, and they never tried to escape. We became so confident with them that we took turns washing in the stream—dunking ourselves, naked, in the clear water, then attempting to scrub the muck off our new clothes—while the other two kept watch. The water was so cold it stung, but it felt good on my sore body, and it soothed the ache in my side where Eadwig had kicked me.

All of this took time, however, and when we returned with the final group of horses, Eadwig was waiting for us. He had his hands on his hips and a scowl on his face and greeted us with a string of words I didn't understand but—from the way Pendragon flinched—assumed they must have been insulting.

"Daylight's burning," he shouted. Those were the first words I understood. "And you're supposed to be working." Squires were leading some of the mares away and loading up others. Eadwig, as he shouted at us, glanced toward the squires, who ignored him. "You've yet to water Sir Fergus' mount. Get it done.

Now."

He strode away then and sat by one of the fires.

"I think I know where he got that belly from," Charlie said.

I nodded, watching Eadwig gnaw a hunk of bread while page boys scurried around him.

"We must move quickly," Pendragon said. "They are breaking camp."

All we had to do was lead the last horse to the water. Pendragon said he'd do it while Charlie and I stayed behind and made ourselves useful. It wasn't a prospect I looked forward to, but I preferred it to handling the stallion, who didn't look as docile as the mares.

"He's big," I said.

"And he looks mean," Charlie added.

Pendragon shook his head, already heading toward the huge horse.

"There's nothing to be afraid of. You just have to show them you are not scared."

"Too late," I said.

Pendragon walked up to the horse and began untying the rope that was looped around a tree branch. The horse lurched forward, swung his head, and knocked Pendragon flat. To his credit, he got up and faced off with the horse, but the horse won.

"He hasn't taken to me," he said, returning to us. "You try, Charlie."

Charlie groaned and walked slowly toward the horse. A soon as the horse saw him, he whinnied, pawed the ground, and reared up on his hind legs. Charlie ran backward, shouting some words I expect Pendragon had never heard before.

"We haven't time for this," Pendragon said, as Charlie ran back-first into him. "We need a bucket."

He turned away, heading toward camp, shaking his head in disgust. "We'll bring water to him. He can drink it, or not."

Charlie followed, but I stayed, watching the big horse. He had calmed down but was still watching me with a wary eye. Then something punched me in the back. I fell forward, gasping for breath.

"What are you doing standing there?" It was Eadwig. "Water that horse. Now." He punctuated this with a kick to my ribs, but at least it was on the other side so now I didn't feel so lopsided.

"My brother and Pendragon are going for water," I said. "They will bring it here, so the horse can drink."

Eadwig smirked. "No, they are not. You are going to lead him to water. Get up and do it."

I struggled to my feet and inched toward the horse, feeling like David on his way to meet Goliath, although David, at least, had some prospect of a good outcome, which I didn't share. The horse stood still, watching me approach, and a quick glance over my shoulder confirmed that Eadwig was watching too, probably looking forward to the horse trampling me.

"Easy, boy," I said, reaching out my hand the way I'd seen someone in a cowboy movie do. I approached him from the side, not wanting to get too close to his head or his back feet. The horse snorted and turned his head but, otherwise, didn't move. I took another step, and another, conscious that, any second, Eadwig might shout at me to hurry up, and that wouldn't do me, or the horse, any good.

"You are a Goliath," I said, when I was close enough to smell him. Then my fingers touched his shoulder. He flinched but didn't try to move away. I ran my hand down his side. "I think that's what I'll call you, Goliath," I said, in what I hoped was a soothing voice.

His muscles were taught and quivering. I stroked him again. Dust puffed up from his dark coat and he seemed to relax. Then I reached toward his head, certain he'd try to bite my hand off, but he stood still as I touched his nose. It was soft, like velvet, and his breath felt hot against my bare arm. Slowly, I took the rope and untied it. Goliath stayed where he was.

"C'mon, Goliath," I said, gently tugging the rope. It was all I could do to cover my own astonishment, especially when I looked at Eadwig, who stared at me with a mixture of surprise and rage. I walked past him, leading the horse, trying to act as if it was something I did every day. He told me to be quick about it, but his heart wasn't in it, then he stalked away, brushing past Charlie and Pendragon, who were both carrying wooden buckets.

"What the ..." Charlie said, his mouth dropping open.

Pendragon stood beside him, saying nothing, looking bewildered.

"I'm taking Goliath to get some water," I said, not stopping. "You two can stay here and make yourselves useful."

I walked on, leading the big horse. Behind me, I heard the clatter of wooden buckets as they hit the ground.

When I returned, a squire was waiting for me, and he wasn't happy. I knew he was a squire because he wore a long shirt, like the knights, only his wasn't as clean and it didn't have Fergus' red-feather symbol on it, and I knew he wasn't happy because he yanked the rope from my hand and started dragging Goliath away.

"You get some fire in your step," he shouted, while Goliath reared his head and whinnied. "I've got to get this beast ready for Sir Fergus to ride, and if he skins me because I'm late, I'll find where you're hiding and skin you."

"You're welcome," I said, under my breath, and went to find Charlie and Pendragon.

By then, the sun was high and warm. The tents were down, being folded by the pages and loaded onto the pack horses, which—with half the camp still not packed up—already looked overloaded.

The knights were gathered around the only fire still burning, drinking from what I hoped were water-skins and not the ones they kept the wine in.

We hadn't eaten, so we begged the last of whatever it was the pages and squires had made for breakfast. They gave us each a small, wooden bowl of something that looked like oatmeal soup and tasted like wet dust, but it was warm and helped me feel less light-headed.

I expected, being newbies and therefore rewarded with all the undesirable jobs, that we would be told to put out the fires, fill in the latrine and shovel up all the horse shit. As soon as everything was packed, however, the knights simply rode away, with the squires following and the pages walking behind, all of them seemingly unconcerned about the mess they were leaving.

"Aren't we going to clean up?" I asked.

Charlie looked around at the scuffed-up ground, littered with garbage and pocked with holes. "Yeah, isn't it illegal to leave it like this?"

Pendragon looked at us as if we had suggested swimming in the latrine.

"I know," I said, before he could recover enough to speak, "we have strange customs in the Kingdom of Wynantskill."

"We should follow," he said.

"They don't seem to care if we do, or don't," Charlie said.

Pendragon shrugged. "Sir Fergus has your cloak, and the Talisman. He has no further need of you."

"That may be," I said, "but we still need to follow them, or we'll never see our cloak again."

We left the mess behind and hurried after the company who were, I was dismayed to discover, not taking the road. We stood on the stone pavement, which was flat and level and easy to travel on, watching as they trudged through waist-high grass and bushes on the far side.

"Where are they going?" Charlie asked.

Pendragon stepped off the road and into the grass. "There's only one way to find out."

I sighed and, with Charlie beside me, followed after him.

Chapter 20

The following days fell quickly into an agonizing routine, which mostly involved walking. Or, to be exact, us limping after Fergus and his men, desperate to not lose them. Fortunately, they could only travel as fast as the pages—and the overloaded pack horses—could walk, so we didn't have much trouble keeping up with them.

Every morning, Eadwig kicked me awake. We'd gather wood, water the horses, and march on in the cold dawn. On good days, the rising sun would dry our damp clothes. On other days, it rained. We stopped now and again for water, and at noon the pages lit fires and cooked a simple meal for the knights while we ate leftover dust soup or stale hunks of bread. Then we walked again until late afternoon when we stopped for the night and the real work began. We remained on latrine duty and, after a few days, became good at digging a rectangular hole with neatly squared-off sides, which we noticed the knights didn't always use. After that, we had to tend the horses.

We weren't allowed to take the saddles and bridles and stuff off them. The squires did that. What they left for us was the feeding and watering. Aside from sleeping, this became, by far, my favourite part of the day. Compared to digging and walking, tending the horses was a joy. All it involved was leading them to wherever the nearest watering hole was—which gave us an opportunity to wash—and staking them out where they could graze overnight. It also gave me time to be with Goliath, who remained docile with me even as he continued to refuse to let Charlie or Pendragon—or anyone else, for that matter—near him. This was as much a mystery to me as it was to them, but I tried not to show it.

One of the trickiest horse-tending tasks was checking their hooves for stones. This wasn't a job we were told to do, but Pendragon insisted it had to be done, which surprised me because he didn't own a horse. Although, I supposed if he had shown up in our time, I'd know that a car needed gas and that it was a good idea to check the tire pressure now and again even though I don't drive, so I didn't question it. What it involved was lifting the horse's legs and looking at the bottoms of their feet to make sure no stones were stuck there. Mostly there wasn't, but when there was, we had to get a stick and pry it out. It wasn't fun for us, or the horse, and they often tried to kick. I worried about trying this with Goliath, but he meekly allowed me to lift each leg and probe the bottoms of his feet.

"What is your secret," Pendragon asked, as he watched me—from a safe distance—lift one of Goliath's legs.

"I don't have one," I said, setting the leg down and lifting another, "he just likes me."

Pendragon shook his head. "That horse doesn't like anyone. You must have a secret way of taming him."

"I don't."

"Believe it," Charlie said, coming up to stand next to Pendragon. "The last time he saw a horse, he ran and hid."

"I didn't hide," I said. "I just didn't want to touch it."

"So, you do know horses," Pendragon said, a note of triumph in his voice. "You told me there were none in your kingdom."

"Not none," Charlie told him. "We just don't use them much."

"But they are there," Pendragon said, "so you must have learned a way to tame them."

It seemed important to him, so I didn't disagree. I thought of the car analogy again, and figured I'd be annoyed, and sceptical, if he jumped into our dad's car and started driving it around.

The other page boys were also mystified, but that made them more curious about us, and less scared, which was a good thing. Eadwig, of course, became more annoyed, and even more so when I learned to wake up before he came to kick me in the morning. I'm sure kicking me awake was his favourite part of the day, so when he came one morning to find me up and nearly awake, he simply yelled at us to get to work and stalked off.

This happened a few days into our march. My feet were still blistered and sore, and my body still ached, but it was getting better, in the same way that if six people were hitting you with hammers and two of them stopped, you'd feel better. I had also figured out that we were heading west without Pendragon having to tell me. I considered this a small victory, even though it wasn't hard. Every afternoon—if the sky was clear and it wasn't raining—the sun shone directly into my eyes, making it so obvious that Pendragon probably figured he didn't need to tell us.

What wasn't obvious, and what he did tell us, was

that we were following ancient pathways, which was why, despite us seemingly wandering at random through open fields, forests, and brush-land, we always stopped for the night at a suitable camping site, with flat, clear land and water nearby. The knights, he told us, had followed the same route coming east, and were now following it back to their main camp, which was near a place called Sarum, where we would meet up with the rest of the knights. I had started to suspect we were following a known path because we occasionally passed—and sometimes camped at—areas where the grass was flattened and dotted with black circles of scorched earth (the calling card of Fergus and his band of environmental terrorists), but the rest came as a surprise to both me and Charlie.

I think this was Pendragon's way of letting us know that, despite my bond with Goliath, he was still in charge of our group, something neither Charlie nor I would have disputed. The other pages might be curious about the three of us, but—due to our odd clothing, strange manners, and peculiar speech—they were still wary of me and Charlie. Pendragon, however, was one of them, and after a few days they began to talk to him and tell him things. Unfortunately, what he learned didn't get us any closer to our cloak, or the Talisman, and it didn't tell us who we were supposed to give the Talisman to if we managed to get it back. But at least we knew where we were going, even if none of us—including Pendragon—knew where Sarum was.

In addition to knowing our destination, he also knew we weren't in a big hurry to get there.

"We are to be at the main camp before the Harvest Moon, but that's many days away," Pendragon told us, as we trudged through yet another stretch of boggy grassland. "And that's why our travel is so easy."

Charlie looked at him. "Easy?"

I would have asked too, but I was so tired I couldn't talk.

"If time was short," he said, striding along like we were out for a Sunday stroll, "we would rise at first light and walk into the evening."

Charlie swatted at the flies buzzing around his head. They left him and came to buzz around me. "So, this is, what, like a vacation or something?"

Pendragon looked at him, puzzled. "Vacation?"

"Never mind," Charlie said.

"When do you think we might get to this Sarum place?" I asked, trying to hide how hard I was panting.

Pendragon shrugged. "They are not in haste. A week, perhaps, maybe more, especially if we stop for rest, like they are doing tomorrow."

I momentarily forgot about my fatigue. "Tomorrow is a rest day?"

"You mean, no walking, no packing, no rushing to water the horses?" The glee in Charlie's voice told me he was suffering as much as I was. He was just better at hiding it.

The thought of sleeping late put a slight (very slight) spring into my step.

Pendragon nodded. "That's what they are saying. The harvest moon is not yet near. You can see for yourself." Apparently, he thought this was also too obvious to explain. "And Sir Mordred isn't expecting Sir Fergus until then."

The spring in my step faltered.

"Mordred?" Charlie asked. "That's the name Fyren mentioned."

Pendragon nodded. "He is a brother knight of Sir

Fergus, and he, too, searches for the Talisman. They each took a search party and agreed to return to the camp near Sarum by the day of the Harvest Moon, whether or not they had triumphed. When we arrive, Sir Mordred will be pleased to accept the Talisman from Sir Fergus."

That would take the Talisman one step further from us. And what about our cloak? And Mordred? Who was he? I hadn't thought about the name when Fyren had mentioned it. I'd had a lot on my mind then, but now I had nothing to do but think, and the name sounded familiar. Had I read it somewhere? Was it mentioned in Granddad's letter? I couldn't recall. All I knew was that it brought with it an unwelcome sense of dread.

Chapter 21

"Lazy dog."

My eyes shot open and I instinctively braced myself as Eadwig kicked me in the ribs.

"Hey," I said, dodging another kick. "This is a rest day."

Eadwig laughed. "Not for dogs like you. The fires need fuel, the horses need water."

I scrambled to my feet, along with Charlie. Pendragon was already up.

"That's better," Eadwig said, "now get to work."

He stomped off, into the activity of the camp.

"I thought this was a rest day," Charlie said.

Pendragon rolled his eyes. "You and your customs."

He didn't feel the need to offer an explanation and we didn't really care to hear one. We just followed him to where we had staked out the horses the night before.

"Let's get the horses watered first," Pendragon said. "Then we can help with the cooking."

It was a good thing it was a rest day. The water for this camp was a stream nearly half a mile away, so it would take a long time to get all the horses watered. We led the first group, washed in the icy water, and led them back. That was when I heard Goliath.

The squire was with him, and he was doing something that Goliath didn't like because the big horse was jumping around, throwing his head left and right, snorting, stamping, and whinnying.

"Hold these," I said, throwing my two ropes to Charlie.

"Don't interfere," Pendragon said, as I rushed in Goliath's direction. "It is not for you to—"

"I don't care," I shouted, still running.

As I got closer, I saw the squire was trying to put a bridle on Goliath, and Goliath wasn't co-operating. The squire tugged the rope tied to Goliath's snout and lashed him with the reins of the bridle, shouting words I believed to be curses.

Goliath tried to rear up on his hind legs. The squire held on and lashed him again.

"No," I shouted.

The squire looked in my direction, surprised and confused. "Keep your distance."

Momentarily distracted, Goliath nearly knocked him off his feet.

"Goliath," I said, "No. It's okay. Calm down."

I rushed up to him. All I could safely get to was his hind quarters. I put my hand on his backside.

"Easy boy," I said. "It's okay."

Goliath settled, keeping his feet on the ground, but he still pulled his head away from the squire.

The squire had stopped hitting him, at least, but now he stared at me. Vertical lines appeared between his eyebrows, and I wasn't certain if he was curious or furious. "How did you do that?" he asked. It was more of a demand than a question. "Did you bewitch him?"

"Of course not. I'm not a witch."

"This horse has a restless spirit. Do they teach you to tame wild beasts in your far-off kingdom?"

"No," I said, stroking Goliath, moving toward his

shoulder. I glared at the squire. "We simply understand the value of kindness."

The squire threw the bridle at me. I caught it awkwardly. The leather straps whipped around my hands and stung my neck.

"Then you bridle him."

"He needs water, not a bridle."

"Sir Fergus would hunt this morn" he said, a rough edge in his voice, "and he needs his horse. If I do not bring him soon, he will skin me, and if you make me late with my task—"

"Yeah, I know," I said, untangling the jumble of straps, "you'll skin me."

"Then bridle him, boy, and quickly."

I rubbed Goliath's neck, wondering what to do next. I had seen the horses with the bridles on, but I'd never seen them being put on, and I'd certainly never done it myself. I ran my hand over his tangled mane, hoping he would stay calm.

"Easy now," I said, trying to slip the bridle over his nose.

"Not like that," the squire said, his voice softer now. "The other way. Turn it."

I did as he said. Goliath stood still as I awkwardly fitted the bridle.

"Pull it up behind his ears and fasten those buckles," the squire said.

"I can't reach."

I had a moment of fright as he grabbed me around my middle, but all he did was lift me up.

"Quickly, like I told you."

When I finished, he put me down. He was bigger than me, but not much older, more a boy than a man, and he looked as scared and uncertain as I felt. He seemed to want to tell me something but couldn't bring himself to say the words. I knew he couldn't thank me. To thank me for helping him would be an insult to us both. It was my place to serve him.

"Shall I put the saddle on?" I asked, hoping it would end the awkward standoff.

The squire nodded and walked a short distance away. He returned wearing a blanket over his shoulder and carrying a saddle. Thankfully, he handed the saddle to me instead of throwing it. "These go under his belly," he said, pointing to one of the straps. "This way forward." Then he dropped the blanket at my feet.

It was only because I had seen so much of the horses as we walked behind them that I knew I had to put the blanket on first. Then I tried to get the saddle on. It was a stretch for me, but I managed to throw it onto Goliath's back so the flaps and straps hung properly.

"Cinch it under his belly," the squire said. "Tight, but not too tight."

"Easy, Goliath," I said, reaching under him for the strap. I fastened it and hoped for the best.

"What did you call him?" the squire asked when I had finished.

"Goliath," I said. "That's the name I gave him. What's his real name?"

"He doesn't have one. He's Sir Fergus' mount, and Sir Fergus has no name for him."

"Then his name is Goliath," I said.

The squire took the reins and began leading Goliath away.

"Where are you going?" I said, trotting after him. "I haven't taken him for water yet. You can't send him out like that."

The squire stopped and stared at me, the vertical lines returning to his forehead. My cheeks grew hot, and a cold knot of fear gripped my stomach. I was a page, and I had just given an order to a squire. I wasn't sure what sort of punishment that carried (I'm not sure the squire knew; as far as I could tell, no one had ever done that before) but I knew it wasn't going to be pleasant.

The squire continued to stare, and the fear crawled from my stomach into my throat. But then I thought: why should I be afraid? I wasn't really a page. I was one of the mysterious boys who had escaped from Fyren and brought the cloak and Talisman to Fergus. I was different, and although that usually meant trouble for me, I hoped this time I could work it to my advantage.

I pushed the fear down, stood as straight as my four feet, seven and a half inches would allow and looked him in the eyes. The lines in his forehead stayed, but now he looked more confused than annoyed.

"You are not of this kingdom, so I will forget your words," he said. "But the horse comes with me."

"His name is Goliath," I said, struggling to keep my voice calm. "And in the kingdom I call home, my father is a Lord."

The squire smiled at this and inclined his head slightly. "Son of a Lord you may be, but in this kingdom, you are Sir Fergus' page, and this is Sir Fergus' horse, and if I do not bring his mount to him straight away—"

"Yes, yes, he'll skin you."

There was nothing else I could do. I stood and waited for him to lead Goliath away, but he stayed where he was, looking uncomfortable again.

"When the hunt finishes," he said, "I will bring him

back. You can remove his saddle and bridle and take him for water then. He will need it."

With that, the squire turned and led Goliath away. I watched them go, wondering who had won the standoff. Since I didn't have any bruises or broken bones, I assumed it was me.

Chapter 22

All morning, while watering the remaining horses, gathering wood, and carting our dwindling supplies of food to the squires, I watched for Fergus and his band of men. They had, after Goliath was led away, taken the six mares we had watered, saddled them, and ridden off. They hadn't looked much like a hunting party. They were dressed in their long shirts with the red feather symbol on them, and they were all wearing swords. Not one of them carried a bow and arrow, or even a lance, and I wondered how they were expecting to hunt anything.

I didn't think about it for long, I just concentrated on finishing all the tasks Eadwig made up for us to do so I could find a place to lay down and sleep. As it turned out, it would have been better if we'd been forced to walk all day.

"Assemble on the field," came a shout, as I was carrying a final load of wood to the main cooking fire. The pages dropped what they were doing and walked toward the edge of the camp. I put the wood down and found Charlie and Pendragon.

"What's happening?"

"Training, I think," Pendragon said.

"What kind?"

Pendragon unsuccessfully suppressed a smile. "Combat."

We followed them to a meadow, just outside the camp, which had been trampled flat. This, at least, made the ground soft; a happy thought because I expected I'd be spending a lot of time on it. I wasn't wrong.

By the time we arrived, the pages were gathering around a pile of what I supposed to be practice weapons—sticks of wood that looked like toy swords, a few poles, like the staff the Druid had carried, but much shorter, and some wooden discs that might have been over-sized Frisbees but turned out to be shields. They jostled and pushed and grabbed and soon each was armed. The squires had them partner up and soon the six pairs of combatants began bashing at each other, either smacking staffs together, or pounding wooden swords on their opponent's shields. The squires wandered among them, shouting insults and encouragement.

Only three of the squires were there, Fergus' squire was not among them. Then I saw him at the side of the meadow, with the remaining squires, each leading a horse.

I gazed around at the activity, my mouth open. Charlie's expression was quizzical; Pendragon was smiling. "We'd better start doing something," I said, "or we'll be told to do something, and I can bet we won't like it."

There was nothing left but a shield and one of the short staffs, so we took them off to the side and practiced swinging the stick and fending off the blows with the shield. We didn't know what we were doing, not even Pendragon, so we didn't get any better at it. After a while I got bored and threw the shield, Frisbee style, to Charlie. He caught it and threw it to

Pendragon, and soon we had a game of Frisbee going, which drew unwanted attention.

The three squires working with the pages remained oblivious, concentrating on the pages they were insulting and, occasionally, hitting. The four squires holding the horses, however, were all looking our way. Fergus' squire leaned to one who was standing near him and whispered something to him. The squire nodded and marched toward us.

"What in the name of heaven are you doing?" He picked up the discarded staff and held it in both hands. "This is how you use a weapon."

Naturally, I was the one holding the Frisbee, so he swung the staff at me. I managed to meet the blow with the shield, but it still knocked me on the ground.

"Get up," the squire said. "That wouldn't have knocked a woman over. Stand fast."

The next blow lifted me off my feet. When the shock wore off, I found myself on the ground again, surprised to find I was still holding the shield and that it was in one piece. The squire threw the stick to the ground, stalked over to where I was lying and hauled me to my feet. He gripped me by the arm, massaging my bicep so hard I had to grit my teeth to keep from crying. "You've not the strength of a milk maid."

I hadn't met a milk maid, but I was pretty sure, if we got into a fight, she'd win. I didn't tell the squire that. Instead, I said, "We've never had combat training."

The squire pushed me away. "That is plain to see."

He ordered two pairs of combating pages to drop their weapons and go to the horses. I was pleased to see that Eadwig was one of them. The last thing I needed was to be paired up with him.

We each got a shield, a toy sword, and an opponent. Charlie and Pendragon faced off with pages. I had the squire.

"Like this," he said, swinging his sword as he advanced. He shouted words that might have been advice, or opinions on my fighting style. Since I didn't understand him, I said nothing, and simply tried to keep him from hitting me as I backed away.

"Stand firm," he shouted, landing another blow on my shield.

Charlie and Pendragon were also struggling, but at least they were more evenly matched. All I could do was keep the shield up and pray I wouldn't get hit. The squire swung again, shouting. "Attack, press the attack."

I held my sword out. It clashed with his and went flying out of my hand. Then he landed a blow on my side, and I found myself on the ground again, struggling to catch my breath. Charlie, Pendragon, and the pages gathered around, looking down at me.

"Are you all right?" Charlie asked.

I nodded and climbed to my feet. The squire came and snatched up the discarded sword and shield. "You'll never be a swordsman."

"I sincerely hope not," I said, but he was already walking away.

We were ordered to go to the horses, where Eadwig and the others were already trotting back and forth as the squires shouted abuse at them.

"Have you ever been on a horse?" I asked Pendragon.

"A few times," he said. Then he looked at me. "You have not."

It wasn't a question, so I didn't bother answering it.

We were called forward and told to climb on the animals. I hadn't seen the others get on, so I had no idea how to do it. Even Pendragon looked uncertain. At least they had brought the pack horses, which were more docile than the others, and smaller. Even so, I had to jump up to land on the saddle, laying on my stomach over the horse's back. I squirmed into a sitting position while the squires snickered.

By the time I was upright, the page riding the lead horse was trotting away and Pendragon and Charlie were ready to follow. Pendragon urged his horse forward, then Charlie did the same, by gently nudging his horse in the sides with his heels. When he was out of the way, I did the same and my horse lurched after him.

We followed the page on a circular route around the meadow, but by the time we were a quarter of the way around my butt was sore from bouncing up and down and I was having trouble staying on. Then the horse went into a faster trot, and I did fall off.

"Get back on," someone shouted. The horse had stopped and was looking benignly at me. I struggled back into the saddle. We set off, and I fell again.

By the time they let us go, all the parts of my body that weren't already aching from the daily forced marches now ached. Even Pendragon looked sore, but he was more excited than we were. He was living his dream—going to knight school and learning to ride—while we were simply enduring a nightmare.

It was past noon, lunch time, but neither Charlie nor I felt hungry. He staggered to his blanket, flopped down and fell asleep while Pendragon joined the other pages for a meagre noontime meal. I sat near the edge of the camp, wishing I could sleep, but forcing myself to stay awake, waiting for the knights to return.

They came back shortly after lunch, trotting into the camp, triumphant, with saddle bags bulging. I had thought they might be carrying bundles of dead rabbits or plump birds, but it turned out that Fergus' idea of hunting was to find a village and ask for donations, which sounded more like armed robbery to me. No one else seemed to care, however. As soon as they arrived, the squires and pages rushed to greet them, cheering, and freeing the heavy bags from the horses. Pendragon woke Charlie and they went to help. I held back, waiting to see where Goliath was.

"What are you standing here for," Eadwig said, pushing me from behind. I stumbled but managed to stay on my feet. "Unpack those horses."

"I can't," I said. "I need to water Gol ... Fergus' horse."

Eadwig scowled. "You need to do as I say." He pushed me again and this time I ended up on the ground. "You will not go near the horses unless I tell you." He punctuated this with a kick to my ribs. "Understand?"

I made a gasping sound that he took to mean "yes," and left me lying there. When I was sure he was gone, I struggled to my feet and limped toward the cluster of pages. Then I saw Goliath being led away by the squire. He looked my way and nodded. I glanced over my shoulder. Eadwig was now harassing the other pages and wasn't watching me, so I made my way toward Goliath and the squire, following them behind a stand of trees.

When I arrived, the squire looked around nervously. "Remove the saddle and bridle. Quickly."

I did it as fast as I could, wincing from my morning

activities. I let the saddle fall to the ground and slipped the rope harness over Goliath's nose, patting and soothing him. He was panting, and white foam dripped from his lips. The squire seemed unconcerned, and continued to scan around him.

"I'm not supposed to be doing this," I said, rubbing Goliath's snout, "am I?"

"It is the duty of the squire to prepare his knight's mount. But this horse … he prefers you."

I felt a warmth that eased my aches. "Yes, he does."

Then the squire said, "I would have you saddle him for me, but no one can know."

He looked at me, expecting an answer. I nodded.

"When we next travel, you will saddle him."

For a moment, I forgot about my bruises, then the pain descended double when I remembered Eadwig.

"What troubles you," the squire asked, in a tone that, if I didn't know better, I might have mistaken for concern.

"Nothing, but …" I struggled to phrase it in a way he might understand, "… we put ourselves in danger, do we not?"

The squire nodded. "Sir Fergus expects his squire to fulfil this task. If he finds me shirking my duties—"

"He'll skin you. Yes, I know."

The squire laughed. "That will pale compared to what he'll do to you."

My heart sank a little at that, especially when I thought that he'd only have to deal with whatever was left over once Eadwig was through with me.

The squire handed me Goliath's rope. "Take the horse. Get him water. When we march again, meet me here, early."

I nodded and walked away leading the big horse,

hoping Eadwig wouldn't see me. Even with that thought in mind, however, I couldn't help smiling.

Chapter 23

We didn't march for another week.

Camping might have been preferable to walking but the people back then hadn't discovered "Me" time. There was no daily rush to pack up, or endless hours of plodding over the landscape, so instead we worked all morning, tending horses, hauling water, gathering wood, building fires, and serving knights, and then spent the afternoons in combat training. Marching every day had been agony, but I had gotten used to it. In combat training, I got new aches every day, and there wasn't any way to get used to that. The best you could do was get better at fighting so you didn't lose as often.

By the third day, as we reported once again for training, I'd forgotten about saddling Goliath. I did get to spend more time with him because I didn't have to hurry when leading him to and from the stream, but I would have gladly traded the privilege of saddling him for being able to spend the day walking instead of being hit with sticks.

"Staff combat," the squire said, throwing the long sticks at us. It was always the same squire. I didn't know if this was his assigned job or if he just liked torturing me. On the other hand, him being around all the time kept Eadwig away, but that didn't feel like an advantage.

"Like this," he said, showing off some moves that were so fast I had no hope of catching on.

As usual, he paired Charlie and Pendragon up with two other pages, and then came for me.

"Hold it like so," he said when he saw me holding it like a baseball bat. I placed my hands to match his, dividing the staff into three equal spaces. "Now watch. Anticipate where the blow will be and block it."

The next thing I knew I was on the ground.

"You didn't watch."

I got up, rubbing my side. "I didn't see."

"Watch harder." He swung again. I moved to block it. He swung the other way, and I was on the ground again, rubbing my other side.

The squire turned his staff, holding it like a walking stick. "Get up."

"I think I'd rather stay down here."

He went back into his battle stance. "Up. Up now. Come at me."

I stayed on the ground, hoping he would get disgusted, like when he realized I'd never make a decent swordsman, and stomp off to play with the horses. Either that, or he'd beat me to death, and at that point I didn't care which he chose. Instead, he looked around as if he was afraid someone might be watching, then came over to where I was lying. He squatted next to me, grabbed a fistful of my hair and pulled my head level with his. "You may be a wizard or a lord," he said, hissing into my ear, "but you have no sense of what is good for you. Now, on your feet."

We stood. He was taller than Fergus' squire, older, with deeper lines around his eyes. He made a slight movement, pointing with his chin. "Young Robert has a liking for you."

I followed his gaze, to where the squires were readying the horses. The squire closest to us had his back turned, but I recognized him immediately. "Sir Fergus' squire?"

He nodded. "The same. He finds you ... useful."

Then he stepped back and looked at me, wrinkling his nose as if smelling something worse than the usual stench of the camp. "I see no use in you, but he is my friend and he sent me to keep you from becoming damaged. If you refuse to fight me, and I neglect to discipline you for your insolence, the knights will find another who will."

I could have been grateful, or horrified, but all I felt was shame. I thought of the other pages, those with head-gashes, broken teeth, or bloody welts across their chests. Even Charlie had a fat lip and Pendragon a broken finger that I'd had to splint with a stick and a strip of material from my shirt. All I had were a few bumps and bruises. I thought I was having it bad, but they were taking it easy on me, because it was clear I couldn't take care of myself.

Without Pendragon's help, Robert's protection and—I had to admit—a great deal of luck, I would have been dead by now. I had no idea why I was on this quest, but I was certain someone had made a terrible mistake. Mistake or not, though, I was here, and the only thing that mattered was the truth of what the squire had said: if I didn't let him hit me, someone else would, and the next guy wouldn't be pulling his punches.

I faced the squire and went into the battle stance he had shown me.

"All right," I said. And the fight continued.

"I beat Ralph in one out of four bouts today," Charlie said.

It was early evening, several days later, and we were leading the first group of horses to the stream. For once I wasn't worried about Eadwig because he had told us to do it, probably because he knew I would have done it anyway, even if he told me not to. He hadn't even told me to stay away from Goliath, and I was looking forward to my solitary walk with him later. I ached more than ever, but I felt strangely elated. I wasn't getting much better at combat, but I was improving, and I hadn't fallen off any horses in days.

"Who's Ralph?" I asked.

"My sparring partner. Or the kid assigned to torture me today. Anyway, I got him good. Once."

I noticed he was limping a little but decided not to mention it.

"I won two out of five," Pendragon said, not bothering to hide his enthusiasm.

No one asked my score; they knew I hadn't won any fights. But then, I was sparring with a squire. On the other hand, I wasn't limping, and I felt a little guilty about that.

After we finished with the horses it was nearly time to start the evening meal. Still, I didn't hurry with Goliath, walking him leisurely to the stream and back, enjoying being with him. When I returned, the squire, Robert, was waiting for me.

"We travel tomorrow," he said. "You will meet me here in the morning."

"I'll need to lead him to water first."

Robert nodded. "Then be here early."

He left then and I staked Goliath near the trees where he could graze and still be out of sight of the camp. When I turned around, Eadwig was standing behind me.

"Did I tell you to tend that horse?"

"No," I said, "but you didn't tell me not to."

I tried to walk past him, but he grabbed my arm.

"And now I am telling you not to. You spend too much time with this horse."

I tried to shake free, but his grip was too tight.

"Then how is he going to get water?"

"I will take him." He spit the words at me and pushed me away. I staggered, trying to keep upright. "From now on, I tend to that horse."

Leading the horses to water was a job one up from digging the latrines. The only reason Eadwig could want it was because he knew I enjoyed it, and he was jealous of the connection I had formed with Goliath. And I wasn't going to let him take it from me.

"That's my job," I said. "And I'm—"

He hit me in the chest sending me backward. I should have kept going, but I came back for him. I saw his fist move and found myself on the ground.

"Your job," he shouted, punctuating his words with a kick to my side, "is to do what I tell you."

He kicked me again, this time aiming for my balls. I moved in time, so he landed the blow on my thigh, instead. Then he left me lying there. It was a minute or two before I felt I could move. I climbed to my feet, wincing from the new bruises, and limped toward camp. It would be time to help Charlie and Pendragon gather wood and light the cooking fires. And in the morning, whether Eadwig liked it or not, I would take Goliath to water.

Chapter 24

The next morning, I was up earlier than ever. The aches in my muscles had begun to fade, just in time for the beating Eadwig had given me the day before to take over. I got Charlie and Pendragon up and we had folded our blankets and gone for the horses before Eadwig was anywhere to be seen.

I wanted to bring Goliath to get water first, but Pendragon said that, because we were travelling that day, the squires would be along to start packing the horses soon, and we had a long way to go for the water. We thought we could save time by bringing three horses each, which would cut out a trip, but it took longer to lead them while holding three at once, so the sun was up and getting warm by the time we had finished all the mares.

"What do you think you are doing?" the squire asked as I ran to where he was waiting with Goliath.

"I had to water the other horses," I said. "I came as soon as I could."

The squire threw the saddle he was holding onto the ground. "It is not soon enough! We leave before long. Saddle this horse, quickly."

"He needs water first."

"There is no time."

I stood, looking at the squire, feeling the sun heating the back of my neck as it rose above the horizon. "I will not allow Fergus to ride Goliath all day without him getting some water first."

The squire's mouth fell open and for a moment I thought he was going to lunge at me and beat me into submission. But then I saw his brow furrow and I could practically hear him weighing his options. He could beat me into submission, but then I might not tighten the girth strap enough, or fit the bridle properly, or even—as he thought I had Goliath bewitched—have him trampled to death. And Goliath was eyeing the squire like he wanted to do it too. Slowly, the squire's mouth closed, and the lines left his forehead.

"Very well," he said. "I think I know a way. Saddle him. Quickly."

"But—"

"It is the only way. Saddle first, then water, but only if you are quick."

I adjusted the blanket, threw on the saddle and fastened the bridle, pleased with myself for not needing any instruction this time. When I finished, I began tugging Goliath, leading him to where the distant stream was.

"No," the squire said. "You'll have to ride him."

"What?"

But the squire had me around the middle, lifting me.

"Climb on. Seat yourself."

I flopped onto Goliath's back and struggled to sit up in the saddle.

"I can't ride this horse," I said.

"Why not," the squire said, stepping away, "you've ridden others."

I held the reins tight, my stomach quivering.

"What should I do?"

The squire slapped Goliath's backside and he jerked forward. I clamped my knees to keep myself upright.

"Don't fall off," the squire, who was already some distance behind me, said. "And do not be seen."

I admit I had secretly wanted to ride Goliath, but I would rather have done it in a less dramatic way. This was the equivalent of jumping into the deep end of the swimming pool and hoping you didn't drown, only that wouldn't hurt as much.

The horses we rode for practice had only one speed—a sort of fast walk—but it turns out, horses have three gears. First gear, a sort of trot, is bumpy, but not too bad. Second gear, however, is so bouncy it's painful. Going up when Goliath's back went down wasn't bad. But coming down as his back came up hurt in a dozen ways. My teeth jarred, my legs ached, my neck felt like I had whiplash and I couldn't imagine feeling any less fire between my legs if Eadwig had succeeded in connecting with my balls. And all of this was going on while I tried not to fall off, which wasn't easy seeing as how medieval saddles didn't have any stirrups. It was just a leather seat with no place to secure your feet. Then, thankfully, Goliath shifted into third gear, which was a lot smoother, but really fast. Scary fast. All I could do was cling on and hope.

I was surprised when he slowed down and I saw we were nearing the stream. It was a good thing he knew where he was going, because I didn't have the time or the ability to steer him. I was so glad when he stopped and dipped his muzzle into the water that I almost jumped off, but then I remember that I wouldn't be able to get back on. So, instead, I leaned forward, resting against his neck, waiting for him to finish.

After he had drank a while, I tugged on the reins to

see what would happen. He lifted his head, and I steered him back toward the camp. I nudged him into first gear, letting him trot along for a little while. I didn't know if horses got cramps from too much exercise after drinking or eating, but I didn't want to find out. Goliath seemed to want to go faster, so I nudged him again and, again, I found second gear to be a painful experience, so I urged him to move into third.

This time, I was ready, and it was thrilling, feeling the wind in my hair, hearing the rhythmic thud of Goliath's hooves, and feeling his muscles work as his massive body carried me smoothly over the grassy plain. I sat up straight, holding the reins but letting Goliath run where he pleased, feeling a rush of such joy it was all I could do to not shout, "Yee haw!"

It was so exciting that I forgot I wasn't supposed to be seen. We neared the camp too soon, and too quickly. I pulled back on the reins, slowing Goliath to a trot, then a walk and to a standstill. The squire was still by the trees, waiting, his hands on his hips again, with the scowl back on his face. I slid out of the saddle and thumped to the ground, struggling to make my legs work. As I gripped the reins and led Goliath toward the squire, I saw why he wasn't happy.

Most of the company were busy. The knights were still around their fire, some distance away. The squires milled around the cluster of horses, some of them saddled, others loaded with gear and food, and the pages were all occupied, finishing up the last of the packing.

No one was paying any attention to me or Goliath, even though we were in plain sight, except for Pendragon and Charlie—who were jogging toward me, shouting for me to hurry up and asking where I had been—and Eadwig, who, even from a distance, looked a hundred times more enraged than the squire.

Chapter 25

The squire yanked the reins from my hands and raised his arm, ready to hit me. "You fool!" Goliath snorted and took a step toward him, which made him drop his arm and take a step back. He looked at Goliath warily, then back at me. "You were not to be seen," he said, his voice softer.

"I wasn't," I said. "Not by anyone that matters, anyway. My friends won't say anything, and I don't think you have to worry about Eadwig.

"They will tell others. If Sir Fergus hears of it—"

"Yeah, yeah, skinning and all that. I'll make sure they keep their mouths shut."

The Squire looked me up and down. "You?"

I could tell he thought I was too small for his type of diplomacy. "There are other ways of reasoning with people that don't involve thrashing them."

The squire nodded, though he still looked dubious. Then I had a terrible thought. "I can still unsaddle him, right?"

He looked at Pendragon and Charlie, who had stopped and were waiting some distance away, with Eadwig behind them.

"Yes," he said. "Silence your friends, and when the day's march is done, come to this horse first. You will tend to him and take him to water."

I nodded, ran my hand over Goliath's side and

started walking away, toward Charlie and Pendragon. And Eadwig.

Then Robert called after me. "Boy. You have a good seat."

I looked at him, wondering what he meant.

"I expected the horse to come back without you, but you stayed on. You rode him like a Lord, as if the horse wanted to serve you. That is a special gift."

I smiled and turned away, wondering how much weight that special gift would give me against Eadwig.

"What do you think you were doing?" Charlie asked when I got close.

"I had to take Goliath for water."

"But you didn't have to ride him."

"There wasn't time. I had to hurry."

Pendragon shook his head in disbelief. "You rode that horse. How?"

"Something is wrong with your ears." It was Eadwig. We turned to face him, with Charlie and Pendragon on either side of me. "They don't hear well, do they? I'll rip them from your head as they don't seem to be doing you any good." The anger stayed in his voice, but he stopped approaching. There were three of us and one of him.

"What is he talking about?" Charlie asked.

"He told me I wasn't to go near Goliath," I said. I looked at Eadwig, "But Robert ordered me to, and he outranks you."

Eadwig's face went red. "I give you orders. Not … not …"

He seemed confused, and I realized that he didn't know the names of the squires any more than I did. And why would he? They were separated by rank and class as thoroughly as if there was a wall between them.

159

I hoped I could use this to my advantage.

"The horse is Goliath," I said, "and Robert is the squire who tends to him. Robert has requested my help, I cannot refuse."

Eadwig curled his hands into fists. I could see he wanted to charge at us and start throwing punches, but still he hesitated. "If I do not assist him as he commands," I continued, "he will want to know the reason why."

Eadwig stayed where he was, still weighing his chances. Then several other pages approached, drawn by the promise of a fight. When Eadwig saw them, his courage returned. He stood tall and faced us. "Now you'll feel the punishment for daring to ride Sir Fergus' horse."

The pages were steps away. We braced ourselves for the onslaught, but they didn't rally around Eadwig; they came to us.

"You rode the big horse?" one of them asked.

"He's a devil. How did you do it?"

"How did you stay on?"

My heart began to pound. Now they would all know. But then I calmed myself. Would it matter if they did?

"Tell us how."

"Are you wizards? That's what they say."

If I could get all the pages on our side, Eadwig wouldn't be able to retaliate. And anything I told them would never get to the squires because none of the squires talked to the pages, other than to give them orders.

"We are not wizards," I told them, because I felt claiming that status might be dangerous, and easily refuted. "But in our kingdom, our father is a Lord. We came to seek our friend, Pendragon, because he is the son of a king."

The boys actually leaned back as they sucked in breath and gave a low, "Oooh," in unison. Charlie leaned close and whispered, "Don't overdo it."

"Were you taught to tame horses in your kingdom?"

"Can you teach us how?"

"Fools!" Eadwig said. "Anyone can ride that horse."

The pages turned toward him.

"You boast."

"Empty words."

"Empty lies."

Before the debate could heat up, there came shouts from the rest of the company and the sound of clopping hooves. The knights had mounted their horses and were moving on, with the squires and pack horses behind them. The pages scattered, following, leaving us facing Eadwig again.

Slowly, his fists unclenched. "It's time to march," he said, mustering as much authority as he could. "Do not fall behind."

He stomped off, and we followed, leaving the usual wreckage behind.

"He's going to find a way to get back at you, you know," Charlie said, sounding concerned.

I nodded, trying not to show how worried I was. "I think maybe this morning clipped his wings a little. If he does anything to me, he'll have the squire to answer to."

"Your optimism is admirable," Pendragon said.

We walked in silence after that. In the afternoon, we stopped and camped at Stonehenge.

Chapter 26

"What is it?" Pendragon asked when, on the far horizon, the strange shapes came into view. At first, I had no better idea than he did, but as we drew closer, the shapes coalesced into a familiar form.

"It's Stonehenge," I said, hardly believing it myself.
"Are you sure?" Charlie asked.
"Yes. I read a book about it. That's it, I'm sure."
"But what is it?" Pendragon asked.
"It's a circle of stones," I told him, "thousands of years old. Even for you."

When word spread among the pages that Charlie and I knew about the strange, stone structure, we were again surrounded.

"You know of the sacred circle?"
"Have you been here before?"
"Did you build it?"

It was harder than I imagined trying to make them understand how I knew about it. The word "picture" didn't mean anything to them, they didn't even know what a book was, and the concept of reading was beyond their comprehension.

"I've seen drawings," I told them, "and my father told me about it." This was partly true. The book of Stonehenge was filled with line sketches, and Dad told me some additional facts about it.

"Did he build it?"

"No. His father told him about it, and his father's father told him, back through the years."

"How old is it?"

"Very old," I said, getting tired of the subject. "If you're still interested, I'll tell you more tonight."

"You can show us tonight," one of the pages, who looked like he was wearing a brown sack that matched the colour of his hair, though neither, I suspected, were their original colour. "The sacred circle marks the way to Sarum. We will camp near the stones tonight."

News that our walk was nearly over, and so early in the afternoon, cheered me up a little. "When we get there," I told them, "I will tell you what I know of it."

As the page had predicted, we stopped near the circle, in an area pockmarked with the remnants of firepits and month-old horse manure. There followed the usual flurry of saddlebag unpacking, tent erecting, fire starting, latrine digging and horse watering. I slipped away soon after we stopped, hoping to avoid Eadwig and find Robert. I was successful at neither. Eadwig followed, but didn't try to stop me, and I found Goliath, still saddled, but tethered, by himself, near one of the massive, upright stones. I quickly untied him and led him into the circle, where I found Robert, having a piss behind the stones.

"What are you doing here?" he hissed. "This circle is sacred. You can't bring a horse in here."

"Well, you're pissing on the stones, so they can't be that sacred. Besides, we're hidden, no one can see us."

I looked over my shoulder. Eadwig was out of sight, but I knew he was close enough to hear.

Robert nodded, so I removed Goliath's saddle, blanket, and bridle. Then I tied him to a smaller rock, inspecting the radius of his grazing area to make sure it didn't include where Robert had been.

"I'll bring him for water later," I said. "I have other chores to do."

Robert picked up the saddle, with the blanket and bridle draped over it. "Bring him back here for the night," he said. "I will hide these behind this stone. After you tend to him in the morning, you may dress him. But don't come into the camp until I join you."

"Sure thing," I said. Then I said, "Yes," when I saw the confused look on his face.

"You won't have to worry about doing extra work for long," he said as he walked away. "We will reach the camp before the next sunset. After we arrive, I will no longer require your services."

"That's ... thanks," I said, trying not to sound as if my throat was constricting in fear.

At the camp, I would lose his protection, and once Eadwig found out, I would be in real trouble. I started back to where I had left Charlie and Pendragon, cautiously circling the rock I thought Eadwig had hidden behind. He was gone, but I barely had time to breathe a sigh of relief when he jumped from behind one of the uprights, grabbed me by the throat and pinned me up against it.

"You don't hear very well," he said, his face an inch from mine, his rancid breath stinging my eyes, "but I do. We'll be in the camp tomorrow, with no one to protect you."

My feet hung inches from the ground, I struggled to breathe and felt myself beginning to black out.

"See how easy it is to catch you alone? And accidents happen."

He let go then, and I fell in a heap at the base of the upright. He didn't even bother kicking me, he simply walked away, leaving me gasping and shaking.

By the time I found Charlie and Pendragon, I had composed myself, but as we led the last of the mares to water, Charlie noticed I was subdued and asked what was wrong. I didn't want to tell him the real reason, so I just told him that we were going to reach the main camp the next day.

"Outstanding," he said.

Pendragon stepped closer. "At last. No more travel. We can spend less time walking and more time training."

"Our routine will change then," I said. "We might not be allowed to tend the horses."

Charlie nodded. "I see. You're worried you won't get to play with your big horse anymore."

I let him think that was the reason, then I realized it was.

Chapter 27

Because we had stopped early, and finished our chores early, and fed the knights early, they were already sitting around a fire in front of their tents—drinking and laughing and demanding that the squires bring them more wine—well before darkness set in, which gave the page boys the chance to pester me into telling them about Stonehenge, as if I was some sort of tour guide.

I didn't mind. The more people around me, the safer I was. Some of the boys were still working, and Eadwig was off by himself, sulking, so Charlie and I took Pendragon and a few of the pages into the stone circle. Strangely, although they wanted to hear about Stonehenge, they weren't at all eager to see it up close. All the boys, Pendragon included, were reluctant to go near it, even though Charlie and I assured them it was all right. We couldn't convince them the circle wasn't sacred, so we told them we had special permission to be there and that seemed to satisfy them.

The weeds around the circle were waist-high and brambles grew around some of the stones, but inside the henge the grass was short. I couldn't tell if someone was tending the site or if it was simply harder for things to grow there, but it provided a definite delineation. The pages grew quiet as they stepped over the line and into the ring of stones, as if they were entering a cathedral. They walked softly, spoke in whispers, and huddled close while Charlie ran from stone to stone, and climbed on some of the smaller rocks, expressing his enthusiasm with words like, "Cool," and "Check this out!"

I led the boys around the circle between the inner and outer stones, avoiding the area where Goliath was tied up, while telling them about the structure, how it was really old and how no one knew who built it. They were in awe of the massive stones, and how familiar the site seemed to me. The truth was, I had a hard time concealing my own awe. First of all, I never imagined I would see Stonehenge, and secondly, it was a lot different from the photos and drawings I had seen. There were more upright stones, topped with crossbars, defining the outer circle, and the jumbo stones that stood in a horseshoe around the central area were mostly intact. The years between this time and mine had worn the structure down, but I didn't mention that to the boys, as it would just confuse them. Instead, I took them into the centre, to show them one of the things I remembered Dad telling me about.

The Altar Stone, which was what I was looking for, wasn't lying flat like in the photos, either. It stood, twice my height and as wide as I could stretch my arms, near the back of the horseshoe. Although it wasn't as big as the other stones, it was obviously special. The side facing the opening of the horseshoe wasn't rough, like the rest of the stones. It was nearly smooth as glass, and the fading light revealed a speckled, almost sparkling, surface. In front of it, set off to the side, was a low, flat stone that might have been a table. A rough area of ground hinted that another had stood next to it, slightly in front of and on either side of the Altar

Stone.

"Hey, look," Charlie said, lying spread-eagle on the stone table. "I'm a human sacrifice."

No one laughed. In fact, the boys—Pendragon among them—looked disapprovingly at him. I ignored him and stood with my back to the Altar Stone amazed by what I saw.

"There," I said, pointing straight ahead.

Slowly, the boys gathered and turned to look, gazing past the opening of the horseshoe, through the upright stones of the outer circle and across a stretch of meadow, to where two smaller, upright stones stood next to each other. In the photos, there was only one, but drawings of a theoretical, ancient Stonehenge included a second one—which was what I was seeing—along with a possible explanation.

"See that gap?" The boys nodded, silent and solemn. "At dawn on midsummer's day, the sun's rays shine through that." I turned to the Altar Stone and placed my hand against its cool, smooth surface. "This stone is not like any of the others here. It's a special stone, with a surface like a mirror. And when the light strikes it, the legends say, it glows."

The boys gave an appreciative "Oooh," then the hushed reverence was shattered by Charlie, still spread-eagle on the table, asking "Is that when they do the human sacrifice?"

With the mood broken and the light fading, we returned to camp. It wasn't late and the knights were still drinking so we had to take our turn serving them. If Robert hadn't told me we were going to arrive at the main camp the next day, I would have found out from the knights. It was all they talked about.

We served them late into the evening, until the wine

and beer and bread they had plundered on their repeated trips to the nearby town were as exhausted as we were.

When the knights finally crawled to their tents the moon was rising, and the stars were bright. We stoked up one of the fires and lay around it, huddled in blankets and eager for sleep. No one was more eager than I was, which was why I surprise myself by waking after what seemed like only a few minutes. I rolled over, closer to the smouldering embers, and tried to go back to sleep, then noticed the moon, low in the western sky, and a glow in the east. Dawn was not far off.

I rose, shaking my arms and jogging in place to warm my stiff limbs. It was too early to saddle Goliath, so I let him sleep and wandered into the centre of Stonehenge. The Alter Stone practically glowed in the moonlight. I sat on what Charlie had called the sacrifice table and faced its mirrored surface.

The moon was nearly full, and this was the one they called the Harvest Moon, which made this September. I had figured that out by myself, without having to ask Pendragon. A small victory, but it was something.

I also learned why we had travelled so slowly and camped in one spot for so long, though not on my own, and not from Pendragon. I learned this from listening to the talk around the campfire. It wasn't like eavesdropping—you couldn't help overhearing, especially after they'd had a lot to drink—and the knights didn't seem to care, or notice, that we were there. I guess, to them, we simply didn't matter.

The previous night, they had been more raucous than usual. They were celebrating the end of their quest—the successful end. Fergus boasted about our cloak and the Talisman even as Charlie and I served him. I don't know if he was making a point of ignoring us, or if he had really forgotten who we were, but it made Charlie angry, and me worry about what was going to happen when we arrived at the big camp.

The reason for the delay was so Fergus could arrive at the last minute. Tomorrow night, the moon would be full, so once dawn arrived, it would be the day of the Harvest Moon. Mordred would already be at the camp and Fergus was making him wait so he could arrive triumphant, wearing our cloak and the Talisman. The idea made me uneasy.

Fergus kept the Talisman and our cloak near him, and there was no way to get them back. Although Fergus seemed unconcerned with us, whenever Charlie or I got near his tent, a guard seemed to appear, so we never even had the chance to look for them. And once they were handed over to Mordred, they would be that much harder to recover. Impossible, even, because Mordred would have our cloak and we would be stuck with Fergus.

Dawn was still a way off and the air was cool, still, and silent. I sat on the sacrifice table, facing the Alter Stone, wishing it could, like the Talisman, tell me the truth.

What was going to happen to us? And what was happening back home? Did time run at the same pace there? Had we been missing for weeks already? Were the police still looking for us or had they given up the search? The only consolation I could think of was that Bobby, Pete and Jason would be suspects. But what about us? Would we, could we, ever get back?

If we couldn't, I didn't want to live the rest of my life as Fergus' servant. Life in this time was hard.

People thought that knights had it good, but their lives weren't much easier and, from what I could see, there wasn't much separating them from some criminal gangs I read about. If we wanted to salvage a life out of this mess, we needed to get away. Now.

It wouldn't be hard. We could slip away in the darkness, and I doubted anyone would notice, not even Robert, as long as I saddled Goliath first. Fergus wouldn't waste the effort trying to bring us back. He was safer with us gone. We could follow the trail back to Pendragon's. Charlie was adapting better than I was to our new surroundings, and Pendragon was no longer eager to become a knight. We could take up farming, live a quiet life. Not exactly the future I'd had in mind, but it would be better than this. Garberend and Aisley would surely take us in.

An image of Aisley cut through my thoughts. I saw her, with that earnest look on her face, bending close, telling me I had a path to follow. Could I go back and tell her I couldn't do it? And then there was the Druid, revealing things too incredible to be believed. And yet we had survived Fyren, and we had looked into the Talisman. All of that seemed important at the time, but now I wondered: could it all have been just random events? Had we really been called or were we fooling ourselves?

Dawn inched closer. The summer solstice had come and gone three months before, but the Alter Stone still caught the light, making it brighter than the grey stones surrounding it. I stared into its glittering surface, searching for an answer that wasn't there. The answer, though I hated to admit it, was with me. What was happening was impossible, but the stubborn truth remained: we were somehow in the dark ages, and we had a job to do. If we turned back, we'd be doomed to stay here forever. The only way—just like in the forest—was forward. And just like facing Fyren, it would be impossible, but we had to try.

I knew I needed to act before the doubts crept back in, so I started back toward camp to wake up Charlie and Pendragon. Then a scream broke the stillness of the morning.

Chapter 28

I ran toward the sound. It was close by. Inside the circle, near where Goliath was tethered.

The scream continued, joined by the thud of hooves and an angry whinny. I raced around the towering stones and saw Goliath rearing up on this hind legs. Beneath him, a terrified Eadwig lay trapped against a large rock, a bridle clutched in his hand.

"No, Goliath!"

His hooves came down, nearly clipping Eadwig's head. Eadwig screamed again and tried to claw through the rock.

I ran and grabbed the rope, gripping it tight as Goliath tried to rear up again.

"Easy boy," I said. "Easy. Everything's fine."

"No, it's not," Eadwig shouted. "He tried to kill me."

I held Goliath back, giving Eadwig enough room to scuttle away. "You're lucky he didn't."

Eadwig climbed to his feet, his face white, the bridle still clutched in his fist. Behind him was Goliath's saddle and blanket.

"You were trying to saddle him."

"I wanted to ride him," he said, his face now turning crimson, "like you did."

"But he doesn't like—"

My words were cut off by the sound of pounding

feet. "What in heaven's name is going on?" It was Alwyn, probably coming to see what was causing all the noise.

I pointed at the saddle and the blanket. "Quick," I said. "Hide these, and stay hidden."

Eadwig grabbed them and ran to where Robert had hidden them the night before. He must have overheard us and thought he'd come early to take Goliath for a morning ride. That he failed, and had nearly been trampled for his efforts, might have brought me a little satisfaction, but I wasn't in a position to pause and enjoy it. I pulled Goliath by the rope halter, turning just in time to see Alwyn rush toward us.

"What do you think you are doing?"

I composed myself as best I could. "I'm taking Sir Fergus' horse for water. We're to be away early. I wanted to get an early start."

"But the shouting. You were crying out like a nursing child."

I put on a sheepish look, which wasn't difficult. "The horse got spooked. I had to calm him down."

Alwyn, his clothing dishevelled, as if he had thrown them on hastily, or slept in them, glared at me for a few moments, then turned away. I waited until he passed beyond the ring of stones, before I started walking, pulling Goliath with me, in the direction of the stream. I didn't look back to see if Eadwig was okay.

I walked slowly to and from the stream, enjoying what might be my last few minutes with Goliath. By the time I returned to camp, all the page boys—including Charlie and Pendragon—were up and the fires were sparking to life. When I returned to where I had tied Goliath up the night before, Eadwig was nowhere to be seen.

I retrieved the bridle, saddle, and blanket—relieved to find that Eadwig had returned them to their original hiding place—and finished saddling Goliath just as Robert arrived.

"You've done well," he said, taking the reins from my hand. "You have provided a great service to me. I will not forget it."

I ran my hand down Goliath's nose, facing away from Robert, not trusting my voice enough to speak.

"When we arrive at the camp," he continued, "the horse keepers, other squires and pages, ones who do not know you, will tend to your horse. You understand that, do you not?"

I nodded. "And what will happen to me?"

Robert rested a hand on my shoulder. "I will not forget what you have done for me. If you remain in the service of Sir Fergus, I will see that you are well treated."

I squeezed my eyes shut and took a breath. I thought, "If?" but said, "Thank you."

Robert took his hand from my shoulder. "Say goodbye to your horse now."

I rubbed Goliath's nose and let him nuzzle my fingers, saying nothing. I just looked into his eye and shook my head. Then Robert began leading him away.

"Never forget," he said, as I watched them head toward the camp, "you rode him. There are few who can say that."

They disappeared from sight, leaving me alone in the stone circle, wondering if I would see either of them again. I rubbed my eyes, trying to compose myself, wishing I could go back in time, to earlier that morning, when there was still time to wake Charlie and Pendragon and slip away, only this time, I would take

Goliath with us. I shook my head, dislodging the fantasy—wishing wouldn't change anything.

I returned to camp in time to help Charlie and Pendragon take the remaining horses for water. Then the three of us spent the rest of the morning searching for wood, stoking the fires, and serving the knights. While we did that, the squires took the tents down, packed the saddle bags and lashed them to the pack horses. The knights and squires mounted and began trotting away before we had even put the fires out. We left a lot more behind than usual, probably because they knew they wouldn't need it anymore once they got to the main camp. Empty wine skins and small kegs that once held beer, which had been donated (stolen) from the nearby village, lay scattered across the trampled grass. Cups, eating utensils, discarded or forgotten blankets and clothing, and a half dozen smouldering fires—the pages walked away from all of it, following after Fergus and his company. And we trailed after them.

The walk was easy, over a hard-packed trail through the grassy plains. The day began sunny, then clouded over, which made walking more comfortable. We made good time, but after only two hours, as we passed near a brook, Fergus called a halt. It was too early for lunch, so instead of scrounging up wood and lighting fires, we topped up our water skins and drank from the cool water. Then the knights took off their smocks and the squires brought them to the brook. I was glad we'd filled the skins and had a drink before they got there because once they dunked the garments in and scrubbed them on the rocks, the water turned as cloudy and frothy as their beer. After they finished, the smocks did look a lot better, though. They were clean, and the red feather looked bright against the white fabric.

Other squires, and some of the pages, polished lances and helmets and, when everyone was ready to move on again, Fergus put on our cloak and hung the Talisman—contained in a small, leather bag—around his neck. The knights and squires mounted up and set off with us following. We looked more like a parade than a group of travellers, so I figured we had to be near the main camp. The knights had discussed it in boasting, slurred voices the night before—their triumphal return from the quest, their lances and helmets glistening in the sun, their uniforms freshly washed, and Fergus leading, like a conquering general, with our cloak flapping regally around him and the Talisman thumping against his breastbone. They would open their saddle bags and show the riches they had captured, and Fergus would reveal, to the waiting Mordred, that he had retrieved the Talisman.

That was their fantasy, but, like a lot of fantasies, it didn't fare well when it met reality.

Soon after, just as the camp appeared, like a sprawling stain on the horizon, it began to rain. It wasn't heavy, just a steady, mild rain, but it was enough to make the newly cleaned smocks look grey and limp. There was no sun for the helmets to glint in and instead they looked dull. And the red plume Fergus had stuck in his helmet wilted and hung down the side of his face.

I had imagined the camp to be a slightly larger version of the ones we had been staying in for the past month, but it was huge. There had to be a hundred tents of all different sizes sprawled over a vast, muddy oval. Men, boys, and horses moved among the tents and smoke from dozens of fires hung in the air. There were wooden structures too: fences surrounding a herd of horses and a scattering of crude shelters.

The company plodded on, but the closer we drew to the camp, the more dejected they became. Fergus tried to look regal when we entered, sitting tall on Goliath, but his sodden clothing and limp plume made him look like an actor in an amateur production doing a poor job of pretending to be someone he's not. Still, the knights in the camp came to greet him, some cheering, others remaining silent. We assembled near the centre of the camp and waited in the rain while Fergus sat on Goliath looking perplexed.

"I have returned," he said.

Charlie snickered. "What, does he think they can't see him?"

Pendragon elbowed him and told him to keep quiet.

"The quest was a success," Fergus continued. "I have the Talisman." He touched the bag on his chest. "Where is Sir Mordred?"

"Sir Mordred has not returned," one of the knights said. He was with the group that hadn't cheered. "You can rest while you wait for him."

It was a sharp insult, and it must have stung deep to discover that, after delaying our arrival to make Mordred wait for us, Mordred had outsmarted him. A low chuckle came from within the cluster of knights. Those who had cheered Fergus now looked at the muddy ground or glanced at the other knights with malice in their eyes.

"Very well," Fergus said, though his tone suggested it was anything but. He dismounted. Robert did the same and rushed to grab Goliath's reins. As he did, Goliath shied from him, knocking into Fergus who got tangled in our cloak and fell into the mud.

The knights laughed, even the ones who had recently cheered him. Squires rushed to help Fergus to his feet, but he shook them off, shouting and swinging his arms like a madman. As he rose, he turned in a circle, cursing everyone around him—his squires, the other knights, the horses—then he drew his sword. Abruptly, the laughing stopped. For a moment, it looked as if he was considering rushing the knights, and everyone, us included, held their breath. But then Fergus, still wild-eyes and raving, pointed his sword at Goliath. "This horse has been a bane to me since we started our journey." He raised the sword, swinging it over his head, ready to strike at Goliath.

"No," I shouted, bolting toward him. Pendragon grabbed my arm. Then Charlie grabbed the other and put a hand over my mouth as Pendragon hissed into my ear. "In the mood he's in, he'll kill you, as well. Do you want to lose your head over a horse?"

Fergus stopped and stared our way as we grappled—me trying to get at him and Pendragon and Charlie trying to stop me. Slowly, he lowered his sword, his eyes now fixed on me, filled with malice.

"Bring the treasure to my tent," he ordered. "I will wait there for Mordred. When he arrives, tell him the Talisman is in my possession." Then he pointed his sword at Goliath while keeping his eyes fixed on me. "And take this horse to the slaughter pen."

Chapter 29

"I can't believe he didn't kill you," Pendragon said.

We were sitting by a fire, eating bread and a thin stew that tasted a little better than wet dust.

"He'd already made a fool out of himself," Charlie said. "He must have realized he needed to salvage whatever dignity he could, and killing a horse and a twelve-year-old boy wouldn't exactly make him look very good."

Pendragon shook his head. "You don't talk to a knight like that. He probably lost more respect by not disembowelling you in front of everyone."

I kept my head down, concentrating on my food, thinking about Goliath. After the stand-off, Robert had led him away and Fergus had stormed off. He had disappeared into a large tent near the centre of the camp and, soon after, the squires and knights who had been on our journey, started carrying Fyren's captured booty inside. It seemed Fergus was going to sit alone in his tent with his stolen treasure, stolen cloak, and stolen Talisman, until Mordred arrived. The camp was large and filled with so many men and boys that we easily disappeared into the crowd. Since we weren't marching, there wasn't much work to do, and so far, no one had suggested combat practice.

"What's a slaughter pen?" I asked.

Pendragon stuffed a hunk of bread into his mouth.

"It's where they keep the animals before they slaughter them."

"Why?"

"Why what?"

"Why slaughter them?"

Pendragon rolled his eyes. "For meat."

Charlie lifted a spoonful of stew, then slowly lowered it. "But people don't eat horses."

Pendragon shook his head. "Of course they do. Why wouldn't you?"

"Because a horse is valuable, and useful."

"So is a cow, but they are slaughtered all the time."

Charlie put his bowl down and looked into it. "You don't suppose …"

I stood and began walking away.

"Where are you going?" Charlie asked.

"To the slaughter pen," I said, not stopping.

"Do not do anything unwise," Pendragon called after me.

"Too late," Charlie said.

I thought they might come with me, but after our long trek, none of us were in the mood for more walking. I certainly wasn't, but I was determined to find the slaughter pen, and see if Goliath was really in it. After that I'd figure out what to do.

The camp was even larger than I thought. There were tents everywhere. Some big, some small, some clustered together, others—like the one Fergus had disappeared into—sitting off on their own. And the smoke. Fires crackled or smouldered in front of practically every tent. I dodged around the other boys and men, most of whom were busy carrying wood or provisions or leading horses, though some—like Charlie and Pendragon—were sitting around the fires eating, drinking, or resting. Just beyond the tents I found a fenced in meadow where all the horses, or most of them, were penned up. The ground in the pen, or corral or whatever they called it, was, like the ground in the camp, churned into mud. But there was a field next to it that had merely been flattened.

I didn't see any other pens—slaughter or otherwise—so I walked to the other side of the field, where I saw smoke rising from behind a cluster of shrubs and small trees. It seemed strange that something should be that far from the main camp, unless it was the latrines, but when I got closer, I discovered the reason for it—it stank. Not as bad as the latrines. It was more of a rotting smell, mingled with the scent of seared meat. I found a path leading through the bushes and came to a small camp site—mostly taken up with a big table sheltered under a tarp—where a man wielding a bloody cleaver was hacking at something that looked like a leg bone.

It brought to mind a movie set for a slasher film. There was blood everywhere—on the man, on the table, pooling on the ground, infused into the mud. That was what I could smell. Piled on the far end of the table were slabs of meat, covered in buzzing flies. The fire was beyond the table, and two page boys, even younger than I was, turned sizzling meat on a spit.

For a second my blood ran cold, but then I saw, beyond the man, a small corral where two pigs wallowed in the mud. Standing next to them was Goliath.

"You! Boy!"

I was so relieved to see Goliath it took a moment for me to realize the man was yelling at me.

"What business are you on?"

"I've come for my horse," I said.

The man chuckled and looked at Goliath. "That one just brought in? I think not. He's a date with the butcher block." He turned back to me and slammed the cleaver into the table. "And if you don't want to be on it with him, you'd best be off before you wear my patience."

"But it was a mistake," I said. "He shouldn't be here."

The man wrenched the cleaver from the table and hacked again at the leg, which was from a pig I hoped. "He won't be here for long. There'll be a feast tonight. I'll be butchering him this afternoon."

"But—"

"Away! Or you'll be feeling the flat side of this cleaver against your head."

I turned to walk away. There was nothing I could do. I needed to get back to Charlie and Pendragon to see it we could come up with a plan.

"Soft on him, are you, boy?" the man called as I walked away. "Don't worry, you won't be eating him. Meat from a horse as fine as that won't be wasted on you lot. The knights, and Sir Mordred, they will feast on his flesh."

I hurried on, wanting to get back to our campfire as soon as I could. But as I got to the other side of the trees, three boys stepped from behind the bushes and blocked my path. They were older than me, so I couldn't be sure if they were pages or squires. All I could be certain of was they were all carrying staffs and none of them was smiling.

The tallest one, thin as a string-bean, stepped forward. "You're the one they say is a wizard."

"Well, I'm not."

"You bewitched that horse," one of the others, with hair like straw and clothes ragged as a scarecrow, said. "The one they call the Devil."

"I didn't," I said, hoping my voice didn't sound too whiny, or terrified.

"Well, the Devil is about to get what's due him," Stringbean said. "And so is this little pup."

I felt like someone had knocked the air out of me. "What? Why?"

"You insulted Sir Fergus," The Scarecrow said.

My knees felt weak, but I stood at tall as I could. "Then he should do something about it."

The last boy, dark haired with a wispy beard, stepped forward. "He did."

I stepped back, no longer standing tall. It was all I could do to not piss myself. Fergus had sent them, not just because I had insulted him. He couldn't allow us to live. We were the ones who had the true claim on the cloak and the Talisman. He had to get rid of us, which meant Charlie and Pendragon were in danger too. I had to get to them before it was too late, if it wasn't already too late. And if these three didn't kill me first.

I tried to speak, but my tongue stuck to the roof of my mouth.

They all stepped toward me. I stepped back. "There's three of you," I said, sounding like I was already being strangled. "And I'm not even armed."

Then, from behind another bush, stepped Eadwig, carrying two staffs. My insides melted. I should have known he'd be in on it. There was nothing I could do. I wondered if I would wake up back in Wynantskill, or if I would simply die a horrible death. But the other three seemed as surprised by Eadwig as I was. Then he threw one of his staffs to me—which I fumbled but hurriedly picked up—and stood next to me, facing my three executioners.

"You're armed now," he said. "I hope you learned something in those combat classes."

With a shout, Eadwig attacked. He ploughed into Scarecrow and String-bean leaving the wispy bearded kid for me. I got into the attack position, and then found myself on the ground.

"Get up," the boy shouted. "I'll not kill you like a dog. Stand up. Die like a man."

I got to my feet. He came for me. I blocked him, backed away, tried to hit him, and found myself on the ground again with an ache in my side.

The boy stood over me shaking his head. "Sir Fergus was wrong about you. You're no more of a threat than a beaten dog. Now on your feet."

The other battle wasn't going well, either. Eadwig was good, better than I had imagined, but he was fighting two and he was already bleeding from a head wound. I got up, and again the boy forced me back. Fighting him was impossible. I couldn't match his skill or experience. If I got close enough for him to hit me, I would be dead. The only advantage I had was my inexperience; I didn't know the rules of fighting.

The boy came toward me again. Instead of getting into his range so I could try to hit him, I gripped my staff like a bat and swung as hard as I could. He saw it coming and held his staff up to block it. My staff hit his and, with a sound like a rifle shot, cracked it in two. Momentum kept it going. I heard a thud and a whoosh as I hit him in the chest. He fell to the ground and stayed there.

I didn't have time to check if he was dead or ready

to jump up and finish me off. I had to help Eadwig, who was now on his knees, fending off the two attackers. I rushed forward, swinging from my left side, and caught String-bean across the back. He grunted and dropped to his knees but didn't go down. It distracted Scarecrow, though, and Eadwig caught him with the end of his staff, knocking him square in the temple. He dropped like an empty sack.

Still groaning, String-bean tried to climb to his feet. Eadwig jammed him in the stomach with the end of his staff. String-bean leaned forward, retched up his lunch and fell face first into it.

Eadwig stood there, grinning, bleeding from his mouth and the side of his head. He wiped the blood away with his hand, looked at it, and smeared it across the front of his smock. "Took you long enough," he said. "I thought they'd kill me before you came to help."

I gaped at him. "Why are you here?"

Eadwig shrugged. "You saved my life. I saved yours. We're even now."

I looked around. The boys were all groaning, trying to get up.

"Best get back to camp now," Eadwig said. "Be safer there."

Before I could move, I heard the roar of voices. Was the rest of the camp coming for me? But the roar turned into a cheer, and I heard the chant, "Mordred, Mordred."

"He's back," Eadwig said. "Come on."

We ran across the field, past the horse corral, joining the crowd gathering at the centre of the camp. Charlie and Pendragon were there.

"What happened to you?" Charlie asked. Then he

looked at Eadwig. "And ..."

"Long story," I said.

We turned our attention to the horses now entering the camp.

Whereas Fergus' triumphal entry had fizzled, Mordred's shone. Literally. The rain had stopped and now the sun returned, glinting off the lances and the polished armour of the knights.

The lead knight, who—judging from the people flocking around him—had to be Mordred, was dressed in a breastplate and helmet made of black metal. His horse was black, his clothes were black and his hair, falling below the edges of his helmet, was black. Next to him, his squire—mounted on a black horse—carried Mordred's banner. On it was the symbol of a black dragon.

Chapter 30

"The Black Dragon," Charlie said.

Pendragon nodded. "He must be the one the Druid warned us about."

There were more in Mordred's company than in ours, but they didn't have nearly as much baggage.

"We have travelled far," Mordred said, "and are weary from the road."

His clothes, and those of his knights and squires, were pristine, and the horses looked fresh, telling me they had done the same as us—waited a short distance away to rest and refresh. Only Mordred was patient enough to wait longer, or smart enough to have a spy in the camp.

"Bring us food and drink," Mordred continued. "And tell Sir Fergus that I have arrived."

A spy, then, I thought.

The squires dismounted and began leading the horses away, followed by the pages. The remaining mounted knights trotted past us, following Mordred into the centre of the camp. As he rode close to us, I looked up at him. He looked the same age as Fergus, but there was more to him. He sat on his horse as if he belonged there. He radiated confidence and—with his head held high and a self-satisfied look on his face—arrogance. For a moment, he turned his head and looked my way. He made no sign that he even registered my existence, but I felt a shiver, nonetheless. His eyes—dark and without expression, giving nothing away—were as black and deep and dangerous as the Talisman.

"Fergus may be our captor," I said, "but he's our real enemy."

Charlie nodded. "Just like the Druid said."

"What are you talking about?" Eadwig asked. "What Druid?"

"The one we met in the forest" I said, continuing to watch Mordred ride toward the centre of the camp. "The one who told us to recover the Talisman from Fyren."

"So, you are wizards."

All I could see now were glimpses of Mordred, as the mounted knights and the crowd clustered around him. Pendragon and Charlie turned to me, looking quizzically at Eadwig.

"No," I said, "we're the Guardians of the Talisman. And we cannot let it fall into that man's hands."

The speed at which they assembled an impromptu, al fresco feast confirmed, in my mind, that this had all been prearranged. It may even have been that Mordred had been back for days, and merely left the camp with a group of random knights when his lookouts spotted Fergus on the horizon.

By the time we got to the open circle in the centre of camp, a long table had already been set up under a canopy, and pages were setting out meat and jugs of wine. I felt a twinge of terror when I saw the meat, but the butcher—now cleaned up; he had either changed or had thrown a clean smock over his bloody clothes—was at another table, carving the sizzling slab. If he was here, he couldn't be butchering Goliath. Not yet.

The horses were gone, and Mordred was nowhere to be seen. Some of the knights began to hover around the table. At an unseen signal, they sat. And waited. The camp grew quiet, and an air of expectation circulated among the crowd. No one moved, no one talked, and nothing happened.

"Fergus is trying to make Mordred wait for him again," Eadwig whispered. "He plays a dangerous game. I cannot think what his purpose is."

The crowd became restless as the expectation turned to awkwardness. Then a knight came out of another large tent, across the circle from the one Fergus was hiding in. The knight held the tent flap aside and Mordred appeared. He had removed his armour but was still wearing black.

"Hail, Sir Mordred," the knight shouted.

"Hail, Sir Mordred," the crowd, like an obedient congregation, echoed back.

"I can't believe he blinked first," Charlie said.

Mordred marched forward and sat in an ornate chair at one end of the table. As soon as he did, a knight emerged from Fergus' tent, but before he could say anything, Mordred spoke.

"Come, Sir Fergus," he said, his voice booming in the silence. "I command your presence."

"Point one to Mordred" Charlie said.

Fergus stepped out of his tent. He was no longer wearing his usual outfit, but was dressed in fine, colourful clothes, like something a duke, or a lord, would wear. They looked expensive, but mis-matched, and I realized they must be items stolen from Fyren that he had put together at random. Topping it off, of course, was our cloak, and the bag containing the

Talisman, still hanging from his neck. He had recovered from his hissy fit and showed no sign of irritation at having been outmanoeuvred by Mordred yet again. He marched to the table and took a seat, not quite as ornate as the one Mordred was sitting in, at the opposite end of the table.

"Sir Mordred," Fergus said, rising again and lifting a silver cup—another item liberated from Fyren—into the air. The seated knights also rose, lifted their cups, and said, in unison, "Sir Mordred."

"How faired your quest, brother knight?" Fergus asked, when everyone was seated again.

"Point to Fergus," I said. "He knows Mordred failed. He just wants to hear him admit it."

Mordred, however, remain unperturbed. "We rode far to the north, and the west, and returned as we had left—with nothing. And you, brother knight."

Fergus beamed. "We found the scoundrel Fyren hidden in his den, deep in a forest. From him, we won the treasure you see before you."

Mordred nodded. "And the thief."

"Hanging from a tree, with the birds pecking his eyes and worms eating his tongue. His stronghold is destroyed. His men put to the sword."

Mordred steepled his fingers and touched them to his thin lips. "And the ... item?"

Fergus placed his hand on the bag around his neck. "In my possession."

Mordred's eyes narrowed. "And your cloak? A very interesting cloak. From where—"

"The thief had this in his lair," Fergus said, fanning the cloak, making himself look like a huge, gaudy bird. "It bestows upon its owner the office of Guardian. He who owns this cloak guards the Talisman, and I own the cloak."

A low gasp rose from the crowd. Pendragon, who seemed to have decided that Eadwig was no longer a threat, leaned close to him. "Is Fergus in fealty to Mordred? Doesn't he have to give him everything he owns?"

Eadwig shook his head. "He swore an oath of allegiance, but his treasure is his own. Mordred is depending on his loyalty."

"Bad move," Charlie said.

But Mordred remained calm and merely inclined his head. "Many congratulations on your promotion. The Guardian has a sacred duty to bestow the Talisman into the hands of its rightful owner. It pleases me that this honour has fallen to you, my loyal brother knight."

I found myself holding my breath. It was what had to happen, and once it did, the Talisman would be well beyond our reach, and Goliath would be the main course at the resulting feast. The crowd watched Fergus, expecting him to hand the bag over, but he remained seated.

"That," he said, "has already been done."

Mordred stood, looking quickly around. "Has my father—"

"The King has nothing to do with it," Fergus, still seated, and seemingly calm, said. "I have bestowed it to myself, as directed by the Talisman itself."

Slowly, Mordred sat. Then he smiled. "You have done well, my brother," he said, his voice strained, "and succeeded in your quest where I have failed. But you have fallen victim to your vanity. The Talisman has beguiled you. It has shown you—"

"No," Fergus said, rising, "it showed me the truth. It's a hard truth, but it's true all the same. I am to be

King. I will rule."

"Fool!" Mordred shouted. "The Talisman is mine. It showed me the truth, a vision of my army, victorious, and of myself striking the fatal blow, making myself King. Your vision is false. Give the Talisman, and the cloak, to me."

Fergus pounded a fist on the table. "No. The Talisman has chosen. They are mine."

Silence descended again. The crowd stared, waiting. Would Fergus declare a coup? Would Mordred order him killed? I didn't have time to think what any of that might mean for us before Mordred made his next move. Instead of shouting or drawing his sword, he rose and pointed a bony finger at Fergus.

"I challenge you," he said. Then, with more force, he repeated, "I challenge you."

Chapter 31

"What does that mean?" Charlie asked.

Already the crowd was cheering and booing, and a flurry of activity surrounded Fergus and Mordred.

"He's demanded trial by combat," Pendragon said.

"They will fight on the field of honour," Eadwig added. "And the winner will claim the Talisman."

We allowed ourselves to be swept along with the crowd, out of the camp, to the big field between the horse corral and the slaughter pen where Goliath was still held captive. I kept an eye on the butcher who, with his pages, was transporting the meats and beverages to the field. Behind them came knights and squires with the tables and ropes and canvass and soon the canopy was up, shading the tables containing the food and drink.

The knights gathered around the tables, cutting hunks of meat, and drinking wine from Fergus' silver cups. More knights arrived. The butcher and his pages made more trips and returned with more meat. I was worried he'd run out soon and need something else to cook.

The crowd gathered in a disorganized row along the field. In front of them, two knights pounded stakes into the ground, one on either side of the field, then they stretched a rope between them. It looked as if this had been done before. The rope hovered over a thin strip of grass running between two muddy tracks, and the tables, canopies, and the area the knights gathered in, had a well-used look.

"What are we waiting for?" Charlie asked.

We were beyond the rope, on the opposite side from the knights and squires, with the rest of the pages.

"The combatants are preparing," Eadwig said.

A short time later, Fergus and his entourage entered the field. He was dressed in heavy quilted clothing covered with a shirt of chain mail that hung below his knees and was cinched at his waist by a braided metal belt. Covering his head was a helmet that, unlike the ornamental one he'd worn on the trail, covered his entire head, leaving only a slit across his eyes for him to see out of. He looked less like the knights I had seen in picture books and more like a deep-sea diver. Then one of his squires fastened our cloak around his shoulders and hung the leather bag containing the Talisman around his neck.

The tightly packed group of men walked to one end of the rope. Then a knight led a horse in and Fergus, with the help of several knights, mounted and settled into the saddle. When he signalled he was ready, another squire handed him a lance. It was three times the length of the staffs we practiced with and, though not pointed, it wasn't exactly blunt. Then he took his shield, emblazoned with a red feather, and urged his horse forward, onto the field.

He trotted in front of the crowd, his lance pointing skyward, his shield in his left hand and his helmet visor raised. He shouted to the crowd as he rode to the far side of the field and back, his armour glinting in the sun. I was surprised he could stay in the saddle, and equally surprised that the horse could carry the weight.

The knights gathered on the far side of the field, the ones furthest from the food tables, cheered as he raised his lance in a victory salute.

Then Mordred entered the field, and everyone went silent. His armour, lance and helmet were black. Nothing glinted in the sun except his shield, which was polished to a high sheen, making the image of the black dragon stand out all the more. Mordred's black horse snorted and pawed the ground as if impatient to start. Fergus turned to face him, and waited.

"We've been out here nearly an hour," I said. "Why don't they just get it over with?"

"It's a show," Eadwig said. "And there is only one event. The knights will be disappointed if it is over too soon."

"Well, I won't be," Charlie said.

Then another knight entered the field. He was on foot and dressed in ceremonial robes. He walked to where Mordred was, then led him toward Fergus, until the two mounted knights faced each other across the rope. I was surprised to see that the knight was an old man. He stood in front of the crowd, holding his hands up for silence.

"That's Sir Bollington," Eadwig told us. "He's the senior knight. He will judge the contest."

Out in the field, Sir Bollington, his hands still in the air, addressed the now-silent crowd. "A challenge to determine the rightful ownership of the Talisman has been issued by Sir Mordred," he said. "This challenge is to be answered by Sir Fergus. The challenge will continue until the Challenger or the Challenged is unhorsed and on the ground. The victor will be proclaimed the rightful owner of the Talisman, and the Guardian's Cloak."

The crowd erupted, shouting and cheering and stamping their feet. The noise continued as Fergus and Mordred trotted to either end of the rope, where their helpers checked their weapons. They signalled their readiness by dipping their lances slightly toward their opponent and, suddenly, as if by some unseen signal, they galloped toward each other. The babbling of the crowd stopped, and the field filled with the sound of pounding hooves.

As they drew near, their lances tilted downward until they were level with the ground. The horses met. A clang of metal rang out as the horses passed each other and the lances glanced off the shields. Neither rider was unhorsed but still the crowd cheered.

"They were too far from the rope," Eadwig observed. "They need to move closer if they are going to get a winning hit."

While the crowd continued to celebrate, Fergus and Mordred returned to their positions. Weapons were checked, drink was consumed, armour was readjusted, and then they signalled their readiness once more.

The horses thundered toward each other a second time. A deafening clang rang out as both lances hit the shields. Mordred teetered on his horse but remained in the saddle. Mordred's men cheered; Fergus' men booed.

"They were hoping Mordred would fall" Eadwig said. "He has disappointed them."

I watched as Mordred returned to his side of the field, sitting stiffly on his horse, his shield arm held close to his body. "I think Mordred's hurt," I whispered.

"That will be an advantage to Fergus," Pendragon said.

And for us, I thought. Fergus winning the fight was merely the lesser of two evils, but it would offer us the only opportunity we'd have to get near the cloak and the Talisman.

I watched as Fergus readied for a third pass, silently hoping it would be the last. With the preparation completed, Fergus dipped his lance, and the crowd went silent. Seconds later, the pounding of hooves filled the air. The horses thundered across the field, the space between them getting smaller and smaller. Slowly, the lances tilted downward.

The lances struck. Fergus hit Mordred's shield full on with a deafening clang. Lances cracked. Splinters of wood flew into the air. Both riders lurched in the saddles but as the horses separated, Mordred remained on his steed and Fergus lay, flat on his back, in the mud.

Mordred's men cheered and shouted, stamping their feet. Fergus' attendants ran onto the field and struggled to lift him while Mordred paraded back and forth in front of his cheering men. He dropped his lance, lifted his visor, and drew his sword, raising it and his shield above his head. "Victory," he shouted, causing his men to cheer all the louder.

"He's not hurt," Charlie said.

"He must have been pretending," Pendragon said, "to make Fergus over-confident."

I stared at the spectacle, not wanting to believe what I was seeing.

Riding to his side of the field, Mordred dismounted. In the middle of the field, Fergus' men helped him to his feet. Then Sir Bollington entered the field. He stood next to Fergus and waited for Mordred to join them. The roaring of the crowd reached a crescendo and then faded as Bollington raised his hand.

"The contest has ended," he said. "The right to the Talisman and the Cloak has been decided. Sir Mordred is the victor."

Cheering erupted again as Fergus' men removed our cloak and the leather bag containing the Talisman from Fergus and put them on Mordred. In the crowd, some of the knights began to boo and others shouted insults at them. Mordred raised his hands and slowly, the cheering, insults and booing began to subside.

"Brother knights," he shouted over the dying babble. "I am not the victor. The Talisman chooses who it rightfully belongs to. There remains no room for disagreement. We serve the same king; we fight the same cause. We have no enmity with one another." He turned to Fergus and placed a hand on his shoulder, almost knocking him to the ground. "Fergus, my friend, my brother in arms, we have no quarrel. Let us unite in friendship."

"What's he doing?" Charlie asked.

I shook my head. "Did Mordred seem like the sort of man to let bygones be bygones?"

"He wishes the bad feelings to stop," Pendragon said. "He wants them all to be friends and not fight one another."

"Yeah," Charlie said, "as long as he's the one holding the Talisman."

Out in the field, Fergus—helped by his men—limped away. Mordred remained, soaking in the adoration of the crowd, still shouting about brotherhood and being united. Then I remembered what Mordred had said about what he had seen in the Talisman. "He's increasing his forces," I said. "He wants to build an army big enough to challenge the king."

And now he had the Talisman, and as long as he had it, and the cloak, the men would follow him. Not only was the Talisman now out of our reach, it had fallen into the hands of the knight we needed to keep it from. A sudden certainty gripped me, squeezing out the terror; this was what we were here for.

"Hey! What are you doing?" Charlie shouted.

It took me a moment to realize he was shouting at me, because I had left the group and was heading into the field. I heard his footsteps coming up behind me.

"Catch him," Pendragon said, also running behind me. "He'll be punished severely if he interrupts Mordred."

By now the crowd—seeing three page boys running onto the field—began to stare. Soon the rising cheers faltered and fell into silence. Mordred looked around in confusion. Then he turned and saw me. Charlie and Pendragon each grabbed an arm, but I shook them off and ran faster.

Mordred's expression went from confusion to surprise to anger. "Seize him," he shouted.

Several knights left the crowd, ducked under the rope, and ran toward me.

"What are you doing?" Charlie shouted from behind. "You're going to get yourself killed."

"Maybe," I said. Then I stopped and pointed at Mordred.

"I challenge you!" I shouted. "I challenge you!"

Chapter 32

The crowd went silent. The knights running toward me stopped and stared. Charlie and Pendragon caught up with me but said nothing. They just stood next to me, as stunned as everyone else.

Mordred looked enraged, and I was afraid he'd come after me personally and cut off my head. So, I turned my attention to Bollington.

"The cloak is ours," I said, with as much confidence as I could muster. "Grandfather gave it to us. And the Talisman has been given to us to guard. We are the Guardians."

"Lies," Mordred said.

"We took them back from the thief, Fyren. But Fergus took them from us. I'm not lying. It's true."

"Page boys do not challenge knights," Mordred said. "You speak falsehoods, fantasies. You never owned the cloak or saw the Talisman."

"They did," said another voice. I turned and saw Eadwig coming to join us. "They speak true. We found them in the wood, where they had defeated the dragon, and captured the cloak."

"Another page boy," Mordred said. "All of you will—"

"I saw as well." A young man stepped out of the crowd. It was Robert. "I was there. Sir Fergus refused them help until they swore fealty. That is against the knight's code. He made them his page boys and stole their property. But they are not page boys, they are Lords, and the cloak and the Talisman belong to them."

"That is absurd," Mordred said. Then he pointed at us, and at Robert. "Take them away and flog them."

The crowd, Mordred, and even Fergus, who was now standing on his own, having removed his heavy armour, began shouting and cursing and calling for punishment. Robert kept still but I saw his face turn pale, and I imagined that Eadwig's complexion looked the same. Then Bollington faced the crowd, lifted his hand, and waited until the roar subsided to where he could shout over it.

"A challenge to determine the rightful ownership of the Talisman has been issued—"

"I'll not contest against a child," Mordred sputtered. "It is beneath my dignity."

"If the boy has the dignity to issue a challenge," Bollington said, "then he deserves the dignity of defending it."

"It's out of the question."

He was in an impossible situation. If he fought me, he would be known as the knight who beat a child. But if he refused, he'd be a—

"Coward." The shout came from the crowd. A single voice. But then others picked it up and it soon became a chant. Mordred turned to the crowd and glared until the chant subsided.

"A challenge has been issued," Bollington continued, "by page ..." He hesitated and looked my way. "Mitch," I said.

"Page Mitch. This challenge is to be answered by Sir Mordred. The challenge will continue until the

Challenger or the Challenged is unhorsed and on the ground. The victor will be proclaimed the rightful owner of the Talisman, and the Guardian's Cloak."

"He must have memorized that speech," Charlie said. He was trying to be funny, but I detected a tremor in his voice.

My wave of confidence melted, and the terror returned. "What do we do now?"

The crowd cheered but, judging from the sudden mob of knights crowding under the canopy, it may only have been because the eating and drinking could continue.

Mordred strode to his end of the field, the cloak billowing around him. Fergus and his men and their gear and the horse all left the other end.

"I think we need to go to that end and prepare," Eadwig said.

"How?" Charlie asked.

Eadwig shrugged. "That I do not know, but it's there we must start."

The four of us went to the end of the field, where the rope line started. I looked toward where Mordred was getting ready. It seemed a long way away.

"You'll need armour," a voice said. Two knights came, carrying various pieces of shiny metal.

"Who ... why?"

"Sir Bollington cannot help," one said, "as he is impartial. He sent us to be your attendants."

They tried putting a helmet on me, but it was too big and kept flopping around. The breastplate also didn't fit, and the padded body suit Fergus had used made it so I couldn't move. In the end, they put a chainmail shirt on me that hung to my knees and slipped off one shoulder. It was also heavy, but it was the best they could do.

While the one knight tried to dress me, the other had gone back to camp.

"Your shield and lance," he said when he returned. The shield was nearly as tall as I was and awkward to hold, and the lance was so unwieldy that I kept hitting people with it.

Then another knight arrived, leading a horse. "Your mount," he said.

I looked at the horse, a bay mare, then I glanced at the tables the knights were crowding around. The butcher was still there. As far as I knew, he hadn't left at all. "Goliath," I said. "I want to ride Goliath."

The knights looked puzzled. "There is no—"

"Here is your horse."

I turned. Robert was there, leading Goliath by a rope. I dropped the shield and lance and ran to Goliath, hugging him around the neck.

"How did you …"

"The butcher wasn't there," Robert said. "I didn't think he'd mind."

I started taking the saddle off the mare, but the chainmail was so cumbersome I couldn't move. It was also too heavy for me to take off. I had to lay on the ground and wriggle out of it while the knights, Charlie, Pendragon and Eadwig looked on in bewilderment. Once Goliath was saddled, Robert helped me get on him.

"But your armour," one of the knights said.

"I can't move in it," I said. "I won't stand a chance wearing it."

"You won't stand a chance without it," he said, handing me the shield. "Keep this in front of you. Make sure his lance strikes it and not you. If he hits you, he'll kill you."

They handed up the lance and I had a hard time balancing it. As long as I kept it pointed straight up, I could hold it, but I didn't dare try tipping it toward Mordred to show I was ready. Instead, I nodded my head, hoping he'd accept that as a signal.

He did. His horse took off, thundering toward me. My mouth went dry, and I struggled to breathe.

"Go," one of the knights shouted. "For the love of God, go."

I heard a smack as someone hit Goliath on his flank. He lurched forward and settled into a fast trot. It was agony, jostling in the saddle, holding the shield in front of me with one hand and trying to keep the lance from falling backward with the other. Just staying in the saddle took all my effort. I couldn't see anything, but the pounding of hooves came nearer so I began to lower my lance. Momentum took over and I couldn't stop its downward arc. Then I heard a crash and felt a jolt as the shield flew out of my hand. I barely had time to register what had happened. The lance was still going down. My left arm stung where the shield had been attached to it. I grabbed the lance handle with both hands and tried to drag the point upward, but it was no use. Then it hit the ground.

It felt like my arms had been yanked from their sockets. I clung on, then felt myself lifting from the saddle as I launched into the air like a pole vaulter. The lance had jammed into the ground, levering me into the sky. It stopped when it was straight up, with me dangling from the handle and the point slowly sinking into the mud.

The crowd roared. Mordred raised his visor and lifted his lance in victory. But the crowd wasn't cheering him. They were pointing at me, some laughing, others shouting. My hands began to slip, and I prepared to let go. Then I realized what they were saying.

"He hasn't touched the ground!"

The laughter increased, but so did the shouting. "You didn't win. He's not on the ground."

Clenching my hands tight, I tried to pull myself up. "Goliath."

He was not far away. He had stopped and turned and was now looking toward me.

"Come here, Goliath. Come on, boy."

He walked forward, stopping next to me. I tried to swing my foot up to get a leg over his back and slipped. Goliath stepped forward. "No, Goliath. Stay."

I swung again and managed to get half a leg over the saddle. Goliath needed to step sideways, but I wasn't sure if that was even possible. Then the lance began to tilt. I edged my leg further over the saddle, then flopped down, grabbing his mane to keep from falling off. Goliath winced but stayed calm. I settled myself in the saddle, taking in huge gulps of air, trying to calm myself.

"I am the victor," Mordred shouted again. "I unhorsed him." But the crowd continued laughing and pointing. The knights at my end began waving and beckoning to me. I urged Goliath forward and as soon as we got to my end, I slid to the ground.

Charlie helped me sit up. "Are you all right?"

"Were you hit?" Pendragon asked, kneeling next to me.

A hand fell on my shoulder. I looked up and saw the knights. Both were grinning. "Well done, boy," one of them said. "You came back alive."

They helped me to my feet. Out on the field, Mordred was still prancing his horse back and forth in front of the crowd, but now Bollington had come out, walking slowly across the field. He stopped next to my lance, which was still stuck in the ground, standing at an angle. He held his hands up, calling for quiet. Gradually, the shouts and jeers faded. Mordred stopped his horse and turned to face the old knight.

"The challenge has been answered," Mordred said. "I am the victor."

Bollington looked at him but said nothing. When he had the crowd's attention, he addressed them.

"The Challenger was unhorsed," he said, "but not by the Challenged." He waved a hand toward my lance. "He unhorsed himself."

The crowd laughed again and, again, Bollington called for order.

"But at no time did the Challenger touch the ground. Therefore, I declare this contest is not over. The victor is yet to be decided."

The crowd erupted, cheering and laughing. Mordred threw his lance to the ground and shouted but it was impossible to hear him. Bollington walked back to his seat under the canopy. Mordred remained on his horse, but he didn't try to win over the crowd. After glaring at our end of the field for a while, he turned and trotted back to his attendants.

One of the knights slapped me on the back. "You've done it, boy. You're still in the game."

I didn't feel as cheery as he did.

"If I go out there again," I said, "he'll kill me."

The knight shrugged. "Very likely. But the minstrels will be writing songs about you for years."

Mordred's men had already retrieved his lance. He

sat on his horse, his visor open, staring my way, waiting.

"You should have touched the ground," Pendragon said.

The knights went out to get my lance. Both of them tugged on it, straining to pull it from the ground, to the amusement of the crowd.

"He cannot be allowed to keep the Talisman," I said. "He's the one the Druid warned us about."

Charlie grabbed my arm and pulled me around, so my nose was almost touching his. "Yeah, but what good does that do us? You can't win."

"Your brother speaks true, "Pendragon said. "We overcame Fyren with cunning and luck. For this, you need skill and strength."

"What Druid?" Eadwig asked.

Charlie, still staring into my eyes, said, slowly, punctuating each word with a shake of my arm, "You don't know anything about jousting. Call it off."

I nodded, but not in agreement. I was thinking about the fight I'd had earlier. That was a fight I couldn't walk away from, and so was this. I had survived that fight, not by having superior skill and knowledge, but by having none. My ignorance had allowed me to fight outside the rules.

"Maybe not knowing what I'm doing is my advantage," I said.

Charlie shook his head. "What? You're talking crazy."

I stepped away from Charlie. Out in the field, the knights freed my lance, the crowd cheered, and Mordred glared. I leaned toward Eadwig. "I need a staff, and a practice shield."

Eadwig looked quizzical, then his eyes registered

understanding.

"Yes, you do," he agreed. "That is your only chance."

Then he ran off.

"Where's he going?" Charlie asked.

I didn't answer for fear they would try to talk me out of it. It wouldn't have been hard. So, instead, I climbed onto Goliath, sat upright in the saddle, and stared back at Mordred.

Chapter 33

When the knights tried to hand the lance to me, I waved them off. I also refused to take the shield. Charlie and Pendragon asked what I was doing but I said nothing. The knights, the crowd, and, I hoped, Mordred, grew impatient. Then Eadwig returned.

"That won't stand a hit," one of the knights said as I took the practice shield from Eadwig. Then I took the staff.

"You'll never hit him with that.

"I'll never hit him with the lance, either," I said. "I'm no worse off with this."

I gripped the shield and held the staff up like a lance. Mordred had pulled his visor down so I couldn't tell if he was confused or pleased. When the crowd saw I was ready, and what I was using, there was more laughter and cheering and pounding of feet. I dipped my staff and Mordred galloped toward me. I urged Goliath forward, into a trot, then a full gallop.

It was easier to stay on him without all the weight, which was good because I had enough to think about without having to stop myself from falling off. Mordred came at me with frightening speed, his lance pointing directly at me, not even pretending to aim for the tiny shield. I rested the staff on my shoulder, then gripped the shield like a Frisbee and, as the point of Mordred's lance got close, I flung the wooden disc at his head.

The shield flew straight toward him, forcing him to flinch and raise his shield. The point of the lance wavered and sailed past. I turned Goliath into the rope to get closer to Mordred. Gripping the staff with both hands, I swung as hard as I could.

The speed of the horses, plus my swing, meant the staff hit Mordred at an incredible rate. It caught him on the breastplate, just below his neck. The jolt stung my hands and travelled up my arms like an electric shock. I dropped the staff and grabbed the reins, pulling on them to slow Goliath and turn him around.

For a moment, the field went totally silent. What I saw defied belief. Lying on his back, in the mud, was Mordred. His lance and shield were scattered in the grass some distance from him, and his horse ambled aimlessly nearby. The shocked silence gave way to low murmurs. Some cheered, but many, it seemed, were not pleased with the outcome. They had laughed and jeered to see Mordred fighting a child, but they had never imagined he could lose. The murmuring grew louder. I knew I had to act fast.

I jumped off Goliath and ran to where Mordred lay. He was breathing, and moaning. I didn't have much time.

The Talisman was still around his neck. I pulled it off and put it on. Then I unclasped the cloak. He was lying on it, and I couldn't pull it out from under him, or roll him off it.

"Help me," I said.

Charlie, Pendragon and Eadwig ran onto the field. All four of us pushed Mordred onto his side, then flopped him over onto his stomach. He began thrashing.

"Hurry!"

I grabbed the cloak. "Run."

Mordred got to his knees and made a grab for Pendragon, who dodged aside.

I ran to Goliath and climbed into the saddle. Charlie, Pendragon and Eadwig scattered, leaving Mordred, who was now on his feet, swinging his sword at nothing and shouting into the air. Then he pointed his sword in my direction. "Get him. He's got the Talisman. Take it back from him."

Only a few of the knights obeyed, but their example encouraged the others, and soon about twenty knights were rushing my way, some of them with swords held high.

Goliath could outrun them, but only until they got their own horses. I couldn't fight them all; I needed to convince them to not fight me. Goliath reared up. The Talisman thumped against my chest. As he settled down, I clasped the cloak around my neck and pulled the Talisman out of the bag. Mordred and Fergus might have been taken in, but the knights, they were only following the leader who they thought had seen the truth. I remembered what Mordred had said about what he had seen, and hoped I was right about it. I held the black stone high.

"I am the Guardian of the Talisman," I shouted. "And I'll give it to no one but the king."

The knights stopped. The swords lowered.

"Fools," Mordred shouted. "Take it from him."

But none of the knights moved.

Mordred ran forward, swinging his sword. "It's mine. I will have it back."

Goliath reared up again, driving Mordred back, but Fergus ran onto the field, also with a sword. "No, it is mine. I will take it."

I held Goliath steady, still showing the Talisman. "To no one but the king," I shouted again. "No one but the king."

It didn't work. They continued to move forward, one on my left, the other on my right. Goliath couldn't stop both of them and I couldn't back him up because the rope was behind us. If I tried to turn him, they'd be on us before he could gallop away.

"The king," I said, looking to the crowd.

A few repeated it back. "The king. The king." The chant grew, but it didn't stop Mordred or Fergus.

"The king," from the crowd.

"The king," from Charlie and Pendragon, somewhere behind me.

"The king," I shouted.

Mordred looked ready to lunge.

Then the sound of many hooves drowned out the noise. From behind the crowd, circling around them and thundering onto the field came ten, twenty, fifty, a hundred knights, all wearing breastplates and carrying swords. The knights on the field parted to let them pass. The lead knight came my way with his squire riding close by, carrying a flag showing a red dragon. Mordred and Fergus stopped their approach and turned to face him. He rode between them, stopping his horse in front of me and Goliath.

"Who calls for the king?" the knight asked.

Silence returned to the field. Charlie and Pendragon came and stood on either side of Goliath. I lowered my hand but kept the Talisman where he could see it.

"We, the Guardians of the Talisman, call for the King."

The knight removed his helmet. He was not young,

like most of the other knights, but he looked formidable. His face was creased and weather-worn, and his red hair showed flecks of grey.

"I am Arthur," he said, "King of the Britons. I believe you have something for me."

Chapter 34

Things happened quickly after that, though, not as fast as I might have liked. If it had been up to me, I would have handed Arthur the Talisman there and then and ridden away with Charlie and Pendragon.

As it turned out, Arthur wasn't in much of a hurry. He pranced around the field to the adulation of the knights, some cheering more heartily than others, before making way for his own company. They poured onto the field, dismounted, and began giving orders to their own squires and pages. Apparently, the field was to become an extension of the camp, and within minutes, tents began to appear. I sat on Goliath, wondering what to do.

All that took place in the space of a few minutes. Then one of the knights who had arrived with Arthur came and led Charlie, Pendragon, and me away. I left Goliath with Robert, with strict instructions to keep him away from the butcher. What happened after that, I don't know, because we were taken to a big tent at the edge of the field and ushered inside.

I'd put the Talisman back in the pouch. The knight made me take it out and show it to him. He didn't touch it, he just looked at it as I turned it round and round in my hand, showing him one side, then the other. When he was satisfied, I put it back and he told us we were to present it to Arthur in a ceremony that would leave no doubt as to the rightful owner of the Talisman, and kick off the feast, which sounded like the more important part of the ritual.

A table and chairs were squeezed into the tent. We were invited to sit, and a squire brought a pitcher of something that Pendragon said was beer but was at least drinkable. After half an hour or so, we were served the best meal I'd had since we'd been there. It made me think of home, and the hope that we might actually be able to return there filled me with such emotion it almost brought tears. I took the cloak off and Charlie and I just stroked it for a while, not daring to believe we finally had it back. After we finished, the knights—there were more of them now, all wearing the emblem of the red dragon—told us we needed to get ready for the ceremony.

It was to be a simple procession, with all the knights gathered, and we—as the Guardians—would say a few words and present the Talisman to Arthur, so everyone could see it belonged to him. Then the feast would begin and the knights—all of them—would once again unite under Arthur. It seemed simplistic, and I don't think the knights believed it any more than I did.

They had me put the Talisman on a small pillow of blue velvet material. Then they dressed Pendragon and Charlie in robes that were too large for them. They tried to have us wear ceremonial swords, but they kept clanking on the ground, so they just let them go out wrapped in the over-sized robes, with me following a few steps behind them, wearing the cloak and a ridiculously large helmet, and carrying the velvet pillow with the Talisman on it. I could barely see out of the helmet, but I did note the three boys Eadwig and I had fought that morning, standing in the crowd lining the right side of the pathway. They were bruised and surly looking and eyeing Eadwig, who was standing with Robert and Goliath on the left side. Further on, Fergus eyed Robert and across from him Mordred gazed at Fergus with a look that did not suggest brotherly love.

The pathway led across the field, which had been crowded with tents, and already the smoke from a dozen fires filled the air. The sun was high and warm. Evening was a few hours off, so by the time darkness fell, everyone would be too drunk to notice who did what to who, and for the first time since defeating Mordred, I felt my stomach tighten with fear.

The knights cheered us as we progressed, but when we came near the end they stopped, and I suddenly felt like I was in church. Arthur sat in a big chair under a canopy, with knights standing on either side of him. His tunic was white, with the emblem of the red dragon, and he wore a blue cloak that looked a lot like ours. He was also wearing a jewelled crown. The chair was on a platform that we had to step up onto, and Pendragon tripped over his robe and fell flat. I watched his helmet bounce and clatter across the platform and caught my foot in the cloak and fell next to him. Fortunately, my helmet bounced off too, and I was able to see the Talisman rolling away and snatch it up before too many people noticed. Charlie took off his helmet and came to help us up.

"You are in the presence of your King," one of the knights said. "Show respect."

Charlie pulled his robe off and tossed it aside. "He's not my king," he said. "And we're doing him a favour."

The knights looked horrified, and a gasp came from the crowd, but Arthur laughed.

"They speak true. I am at their service." He looked

at Charlie. "You are the one they call Charlie, are you not?" Charlie nodded. "Impetuous and brave. This is what I am told."

Charlie shrugged. "Whatever."

"And Mitch." Arthur looked at me, and then with an unsettling longing at the Talisman. "The unlikely warrior. They say you are a wizard who talks to horses and fights with the strength of many men."

"Um, none of that's true," I told him, but he had already moved on to Pendragon.

"You share my name, boy. I am Arthur Pendragon, son of Uther Pendragon. I would be honoured to have you as a squire."

"Sir," Pendragon said, almost tripping over his words, "Your Highness, My Lord." He stopped and quickly knelt. "I do not think knighthood suits me. I am but a humble farmer and I wish nothing more than to return to my farm."

Arthur smiled. "Rise, young Pendragon. Your decision grieves me, yet I feel we shall meet again."

Pendragon stood but kept his head bowed.

"You are the Guardians of the Talisman," Arthur said. "The Talisman belongs to me but was stolen by a cunning thief. You have valiantly won it back, and for this I am in your debt."

His brief account glossed over a number of details, but I wasn't going to argue. I assumed this was the part where I was supposed to say something, but no one had told me what, so I just held up the pillow and let Arthur take the Talisman. He stood, then held it up for the crowd to see.

"The Talisman is mine once more," he said. "The Land is safe; the kingdom is secure."

Then the words came to me. I don't know why or

from where, but I knew it was what I needed to say.

"You do not own the Talisman," I said, as loud as I could. Low gasps from the crowd assured me that I as being heard. "You are but a custodian. Look into it with an honest heart and use its power wisely."

The gasps turned to a murmur and then a half-hearted cheer. Arthur smiled, but he looked annoyed. He raised his hands, addressing the crowd. "The feast," he said, and the cheering became a roar.

"You will dine as my guests," Arthur said, "and sit at my table."

I looked around at the crowd. Despite Arthur's all-for-one-and-one-for-all attitude, I didn't feel confident in our safety. His was a brutal world and, although I didn't doubt his sincerity, his protection could not extend to every dark corner. And, as Eadwig had not long ago impressed upon me, accidents happen. And besides, I was in a hurry to get back home.

"I fear that won't be possible," I said.

Arthur frowned.

From behind, Charlie said, "Mitch, there'll be food—good food—and beer."

"Our task here is finished," I said, ignoring Charlie. "It's time for us to leave."

Chapter 35

For a King we had twice told something he didn't want to hear, Arthur was accommodating. He ordered two of his knights to prepare for a journey and within the hour, Charlie, Pendragon, and I were riding out of the camp, with me on Goliath, following the knights—Sir Leland and Sir Barlow—and accompanied by Robert and Eadwig.

As twilight settled, we arrived back where we had started from that morning and, for a second night in a row, camped within sight of Stonehenge before moving on at first light. With a smaller group, all mounted, we made good time, following the trail we had marked on our way west. Riding was easier than walking so, despite having sore butts, it was almost enjoyable. Near noon on our fourth day, we reached the road where Fergus and his company had camped on our first day of captivity.

Instead of retracing our route through the forest, we followed the road, which, after a few miles, led us to a stone bridge and mounds of earth that looked like ruined buildings. From there, we took a smaller road, leading east. Within a mile, the road became narrow, indistinct, and riddled with potholes. It also began to look familiar. Pendragon spotted it first.

"This is the road to Horsham," he said, trying to urge his horse past Barlow. "My mother, my father, they will want to see me."

"You've been dead to them for weeks," Barlow said. "A few more minutes won't hurt."

Near town, the road widened, and we rode two abreast into the muddy yard outside of Steric's public house.

"I know my way home," Pendragon said. "Can I take your leave?"

"Other's will be glad of your return, as well," Leland said, as Barlow dismounted and went inside. "Better to bring them all here instead of you running to each of them."

A minute later a woman ran out, followed by Steric. The woman ran to Pendragon and dragged him from his horse, locking him in a fierce hug.

"We thought you dead," Steric said, grabbing Pendragon by an arm. Then he looked at Charlie and me. "You, as well? By the gods."

He spread his arms out and turned one way, then the other, as if at a loss. "We must welcome you, and honour those who brought you to us."

Pendragon, still locked in the woman's embrace, said nothing. We all dismounted. Several men and a group of boys of various ages came from inside the pub. The boys took our horses and two were sent running in different directions with the news. Cups of beer were handed to us as more people flooded into the yard.

It wasn't long before Aisley and Garberend came running. Pendragon had just been released from yet another embrace when his father enfolded him in a bear hug, sobbing openly. Aisley, on the other hand, was markedly calm. She hugged Pendragon when she got the chance, then led him away while Garberend and the rest of the village men gathered around Barlow and Leland, drinking beer, and encouraging them to tell their stories. Despite Charlie and I being in a hurry to get back home, she took us to Pendragon's, where she served us a tasty stew, then told us to sleep while she took our clothes, and the cloak, to wash them.

It was a ludicrous idea. There was no way I was going to sleep but, as soon as my head hit the mat, the events of the past weeks caught up with me and I was away. When we woke sometime later, Aisley presented us with our cleaned clothes, and I saw what she had done. She was preparing us for our trip home, dressing us as we had been when we first arrived. It felt odd and made me sad, excited, and slightly homesick.

I thought she was going to let Pendragon take us back to where we had first met him, so we could try to find our way to the holly bushes, but instead she took us to the village square where we had encountered Fyren.

I can't say much for medieval life. It's dirty and boring and smelly, but they do like a party. I guess, when you haven't got much to look forward to, anything is an excuse, and our return merited a huge celebration. The square was packed with tables of food and drink, and everyone in town, it seemed, was there, laughing and drinking and slapping Garberend on the back and crowding around the knights and Robert and Eadwig, eager for their stories. Until we arrived. Then they surged toward us but, fortunately, it was Pendragon who was caught in the tide. They carried him to one of the tables, sat him in a chair and asked him a hundred questions at once while we stood off to one side watching.

"Don't you want to go to him?" I asked.

Aisley, gazing at her son, shook her head. "I will have him for the rest of my life. The village was saddened by his death. Let them rejoice in his return."

I stood next to her, along with Charlie, feeling awkward. She had carried our cloak to the square and I was eager to get it back.

"Should we be on our way now?"

Again, she shook her head.

"Not yet. Celebrate first, then take your leave."

So, we did. We were ushered to a table and seated next to Eadwig and Robert, across from Barlow and Leland, with Pendragon at the head. Meat, cheese, bread, beans, and beer—lots of beer—found its way to us. Pendragon told his story over and over, embellishing a little more each time but keeping, mostly, to the truth. At least he credited me with defeating Mordred, a tale the knights added their own observations to. I was slapped on the back so many times my shoulder blades went numb. Garberend gave Charlie and me simultaneous, one-armed hugs around the neck that almost choked me. "I knew there was something special about you two as soon as I saw you." And I'm sure he believed it.

Aisley, sitting near the far end of the long table, beamed.

As the afternoon wore on and the air grew chilly, a fire was lit and we all gathered around it, drinking, singing, and dancing. As the shadows grew long, the dancing and singing grew more raucous and I began to doubt we would get back to where we needed to be that evening but, strangely, I didn't care. I took another gulp of beer and tried, along with Charlie to pick up the chorus of the song they were singing.

"For the first time since we've been here," I said to

Charlie, surprised at how thick my tongue felt, "I'm having a good time."

Charlie leaned against me. "I hate to admit it," he said, his voice unnaturally loud, "but I don't care if we ever get home."

Then someone draped the cloak over our shoulders. "It is time."

I turned, expecting to see Aisley, but it was the Druid.

"But this is our party," Charlie said, holding up his cup.

I looked to where Pendragon, Eadwig and Robert were, all of them laughing and singing with the others.

"You are but shadows now, "the Druid said. "This is their time. You must return to yours."

I pulled the cloak off, bundled it up and we turned to go. No one noticed, or tried to stop us, or said goodbye. But in the dim light at the edge of the square, where the main street began, Aisley waited in the shadows.

She knelt in the mud and pulled us both into a hug. "You did not turn away," she whispered. "And you brought my son back to me. I will not forget you, brothers from a strange land who travel with a cloak and ride carriages in the air."

She released us then and the Druid led us through the deserted street. Soon, the din of the celebration faded and, as we left the town, all was silent and still and night was drawing in. I trudged on behind the Druid with Charlie at my side, feeling as tired as on the trek west, only now I had the bundled cloak clutched to my chest, and I wasn't hungry or cold or terrified. I thought of all we had been through, and how—even though we hadn't turned away, as Aisley noted—we still couldn't have done it without a lot of luck. If Arthur hadn't shown up when he did, things would have turned out differently, and the three of us together couldn't have stopped that. We'd managed to get into Fyren's hideout, thanks to the Druid, but he'd been no help in the fight against Mordred. Then a thought came to me.

"You sent the king," I said. "That's why you couldn't stay in the woods with us. You knew what was going to happen."

The Druid said nothing, but he slowly nodded his head.

We walked out on the same road we had ridden in on, but we didn't follow the path we had taken with Pendragon. The Druid kept walking until, somewhere further on, he turned down a narrow track I hadn't noticed before. It looked as if it had, at one time, been a road, but now it was merely a path, difficult to negotiate in the gloom. A short time later, we left the path, walked into the woods, and found the ring of holly bushes. If Charlie and I had gone in the opposite direction, we would have found the path instead of Pendragon. But would things have turned out the same if we had?

"Is this the entrance?" I asked. "The place we needed to mark if we wanted to return home?"

"It is."

"So, we're really going home?" Charlie asked.

I suddenly felt sad. I hadn't thought about home in so long and had given up the idea that I would ever get back. But now that I was going all I could think was that I had not said goodbye to Pendragon, Eadwig, Robert, or Goliath.

The Druid looked down at me. "They will not

forget you," he said, even though I hadn't uttered a word. "And you will not forget them."

The Druid walked into the ring, passing through the holly as if he were stepping from one room to another. We followed close and found ourselves standing in the small circle.

"Lay as you were when you arrived," the Druid said. "And cover yourselves with the cloak."

"That's it?" I asked. "That will take us home?"

The Druid nodded.

"But what will we find?" Charlie asked. "It's been weeks."

"Mere moments have passed in your world," the Druid said. "You will return to what you left. You need only be prepared for that."

We laid down and I arranged the cloak over us.

"It was kinda like this, right?"

"Yeah," Charlie said. "As near as I can remember. It's been a while. What were we doing when we left?"

Strangely, I felt myself spinning, and sinking into darkness.

"We were in the woods … mom was going to call us for lunch …"

When Charlie spoke, his voice sounded far away. "You were afraid we'd get in trouble because we'd left the yard when she told us not to."

"You left the yard," I said. "I just followed … we needed to get the cloak … we followed those boys … Pete … Jason … and …"

Then the darkness overtook me.

Chapter 36
June 2013

"… Bobby!"

I whipped the cloak away. Daylight filtered through the trees, making me squint. Bobby stood over us, looking down. I elbowed Charlie, jumped to my feet, and almost fell over. My head pounded and the world spun for a moment.

"There they are. Get them, Bobby"

It was Pete and Jason, running toward us. Charlie rushed them, diving headfirst into Jason's stomach. I moved away from Bobby, even though he didn't seem to be coming at me. I dropped the cloak on the ground and stood in front of it. Pete stopped a few feet away.

"I'm taking that," he said. "Your only choice is whether I go through you to get it."

"Your choice is whether you walk away, or limp," I said.

A look of uncertainty crossed Pete's face. Then he lunged.

I blocked his punch with my arm and, as he blocked my fist with his other hand, so I kicked him in the shin.

"Ow. Why you—"

I punched him, hard, in the stomach. He staggered back a few paces, but I knew he hadn't given up. I grabbed a stick. It wasn't as long, or straight, as the staffs we'd practiced with, but it was better than trying to match him with my fists. I had surprised him once; he wouldn't fall for that again.

"Oh, you're looking for a real beating," Pete said, grabbing another stick. His was longer than our practice staffs, and thicker, and almost as unwieldy as the jousting lance. He swung it at me, but I easily dodged back out of range. As soon as it swung past, and before he could swing it back, I jumped forward, giving him a one-two strike: a hit to the left kidney and the right shoulder. Pete grunted and dropped the stick. I turned the staff like I had been taught, stuck it between his legs and tripped him.

He fell on his back and before he could get up, I held the staff against the base of his neck, not putting any pressure on it, but discouraging him from moving. Nearby, Charlie had Jason in a headlock and was rubbing his face in the dirt.

"What do you say, Charlie? Should we let them go?"

Charlie released Jason. I stepped back but kept the staff. Jason and Pete stood, Pete favouring his left leg and Jason bleeding from his nose.

"C'mon, Bobby," Jason said. "These guys aren't worth it. Let's go."

Without waiting, they left. I was pleased to see Pete was limping. That left only Bobby. We both turned, ready to continue the fight, but Bobby just stood, staring, his face white.

"You all right, Bobby," I asked.

Bobby stayed where he was, as if he was afraid to come near us. "You fell through the ground," he said. "I ... you were under that blanket. You fell and ... disappeared. Then you came back."

I dropped the staff and picked up the cloak. "You know, Bobby. Sometimes our eyes play tricks on us."

"Yeah, go home," Charlie said, "have something to eat. You'll feel better."

"But you ... Pete ... Jason ..."

"It would probably be a good idea if you didn't say anything about this. Just forget it happened. We'll see you later, okay?"

Bobby nodded and walked away, his face still white.

As soon as we were alone, Charlie sat heavily on a log and stared into the trees. "That was ... what happened?"

I turned in a circle, scanning the familiar wood. Being there felt as surreal as finding ourselves in the forest outside of Horsham. "I don't know. I had a dream; we were in the olden days."

"If it was a dream," Charlie said. "I think I had the same one. Remember Pendragon?"

I nodded. "And Fergus, and Goliath?"

"We rode horses and washed in streams and shit in the woods."

"But we're home now," I said. "And we might be able to get back in the yard before Mom finds out we're gone."

"Strange to have that to worry about instead of, say, being roasted alive."

"Or getting skewered by a jousting lance."

Charlie nodded. "What did you mean about seeing Bobby later?"

I took a deep breath—tasting the faint tang of car exhaust—and sat down next to Charlie. "I thought, if we ever got home, I'd want nothing more than to sleep for a week. But I feel strangely ... energized."

Charlie stood up and paced. "Yeah, I get it. I feel okay too. But we still need to get home."

"After lunch, though," I said, grinning up at Charlie.

"I really don't feel like sitting around the house listening to Mom and Dad bicker. So, let's go back to batting practice."

Charlie looked surprised. "Really?"

I stood up. "Really." We walked away, side by side, heading for home. "I think I might be able to hit Bobby's fast ball now."

Acknowledgments

I need to thank my grandsons, Mitch and Charlie, whose births sparked in me the original idea. The simple tale I wove for them, when they were still far too young to read it, was the genesis of this story.

The Talisman—a series of eight books—grew from that original, one-off fairy tale. *The Magic Cloak* is the first instalment in the series.

About the Author

Michael Harling is originally from upstate New York. He moved to Britain in 2002 and currently lives in Sussex.

Lindenwald Press
Sussex, United Kingdom

Printed in Great Britain
by Amazon